The

PROTECTOR

of

DUNBAR

The

PROTECTOR

of

DUNBAR

Eric Ferguson

credo
house publishers

Published in the United States of America by Credo House Publishers,
a division of Credo Communications, LLC, Grand Rapids, Michigan
credohousepublishers.com

ISBN: 978-1-62586-277-8

Front and back cover illustrations by John Taylor
Cover and interior design by Believe Book Design
Editing by Nycole Sinks

Printed in the United States of America

First edition

ONE

The Invasion

Sara opened her eyes and was confused. It was the middle of the night and pitch black in her room when she heard someone banging on the door. She raised her body up and heard yelling from the hallway. "What is going on out there?" Sara muttered. "Why is someone waking me up at this time of night?"

"My lady, my lady, please get up!" yelled Fergus.

Sara bolted out of bed and grabbed a shawl to wrap around her. She ran toward the door and swung it open.

"WE ARE UNDER ATTACK, MY LADY!" yelled her husband's oldest son Fergus.

Sara was not fully awake and stared at the Prince of Dunbar.

"What? Who? Are you sure?" Sara asked dumbfounded.

As she was speaking, Sara could see men and women running through the corridors. There were loud booms and shouts reverberating throughout the castle, and it sounded as if the castle itself was groaning.

"We don't know who this enemy is, but we are under attack! Follow me to the war room, my lady. We need to meet with our council quickly to save our people!" Fergus loudly proclaimed.

"Ok, let's move swiftly," Sara replied.

As Sara and Fergus were rushing toward the war room in the dark corridors of the castle, she could see men and women in their nightclothes running frantically. A woman known to Sara as Isla tried stopping her, but Fergus pushed her aside and shouted at her to leave the queen alone. Sara looked back at Isla and could see the terror on her face. There was blood trickling down Isla's face as she stared back at the queen. Several Dunbarians were lying on the floor with flesh wounds as Sara hustled along the corridors. People were in shock; how could the mighty Dunbar be surprised like this?

They reached the war room and the two guards stepped aside so Fergus could open the large, dark door. Sara walked into the room and looked up to see Finn (cousin to Andrew), Timothy (the second in command of the royal guards), Scott (the commanding royal guard), Eamon (acting head priest), and Angus (the general of the king's army). Each man stood up when they saw the queen enter the room. Fergus guided the queen to her seat, and she sat down. As she looked around the room at the king's councilmen, she sensed their trepidation.

Scott stood up and faced the queen. "My lady, let me fill you in on what we know. An unknown army approached our castle and orchestrated an attack. This army started by targeting the walls protecting the draw-bridge between the moats. Their archers have been shooting lit arrows into the lower keep of the castle. They have catapults that have been pounding the castle walls with large boulders. Several fires have occurred inside the castle itself, and several people have been killed while others have been wounded. We have been busy fortifying the outer walls and putting the fires out. We have also mustered our archers to counterattack. It is so dark out tonight it is hard to tell the numbers of our enemy, but based on some eyewitness accounts, it looks to be immense."

Sara looked to the war council for comfort, but the worry etched on their faces provided none.

She asked, "Since we don't know who is attacking us, how many men they have, or how far they've advanced on our outer gate, what do you suggest we do to fight back?"

Fergus stood up and addressed the people in the room, "I think the first thing we need to do is get the counterattack working efficiently. We need to get our catapults and archers on top of the moat walls to rain down on the enemy. This will provide cover for our army to assemble and plan. Finally, Eamon should coordinate our hospital so the wounded can be tended to.

After we stop the invasion, I can lead our army in an attack against them. With several more hours of darkness, we are limited in our countermeasures, but we can't let them break through our defenses and enter the castle. That would be devasting!"

The men all nodded their heads in agreement and looked at the queen.

"Is there any other way to enter the castle besides breaking through the doors and crossing the two moats?" Sara asked.

Scott replied, "No, my queen. This castle is impenetrable. There is no way to go under or behind the castle due to the mountains surrounding us. The wet and dry moats provide further protection. The only way is for the enemy to break down the walls surrounding the moats and come straight into the castle. It is crucial we provide more defenses immediately to those walls."

Finn spoke up, "It would be better if Andrew was here. I wish there was a way to reach him. At our kingdom's greatest hour, he is not here to protect us!"

Sara looked indignantly at Finn. "You know, Finn, it doesn't do any good wasting time on matters such as this. We must use the resources and manpower to save the people inside this castle. Does everyone agree that Fergus's plan is the best course of action?"

They all nodded in agreement. "Ok, then it is settled," the queen declared. "Eamon, go gather your men to set up the hospital. Angus and Fergus muster the army for battle. Timothy, assess the defenses of the moats, and Scott will make sure our catapults and archers are raining down fire on the enemy. Finn, you will come with me to the lookout tower so I can determine the enemy's numbers. We will reconvene at dawn to assess the situation. If there is a breach in our defenses ring the alarm bell so we can close off the main keep. May God keep us and our people safe. Go, go now!"

The men all jumped up and ran out of the room. Finn looked over at Sara and their eyes met. For the first time since the meeting had started, Finn could sense fear in Sara's eyes. As the two were exiting the room, a large explosion shook the entire castle.

Sara was jolted and fell into Finn. Finn grabbed her and pulled her along as they went up the stairs toward the observation tower at the top of the castle. The stairs were steep, narrow, and very poorly lit. Cobwebs hit their faces as they hurriedly climbed farther and farther up. After at least ten minutes, the two reached the observation tower. This was the tallest part of the castle in which a person could stand. The room, around one hundred feet in diameter, had worn wooden floors and a few wooden chairs scattered around. On a typical clear night, you could see stars and planets in the sky, but tonight was overcast, so there was very little light to see with.

Finn lit the two lanterns, and Sara approached the edge of the room. As she looked out, the clouds parted and moonlight pierced through the gloomy night. Sara and Finn could now see with little difficulty. Sara gasped as she, for the first time, saw the enormous army that was attacking the castle. Legions and legions of men, some on horseback and others infantry, were spread out for what seemed like miles.

The enemy was laying bridges across the outer moat that protected Dunbar's castle. On top of those bridges, she could see engineers placing ladders down so they could scale the wall. Their archers were shooting up at Dunbarian guards on top of the walls. The Dunbarian guards were throwing hot tar and rocks on top of the enemy. Men were flailing about, screaming in terror, and falling into the crocodile-filled moat. The crocodiles were latching onto men from both armies and dragging them deeper into the water. The enemy's catapults were shooting immense boulders that crashed into the castle walls, causing parts of the exterior wall to crack. Sara had never seen an army this big, not even the Odoran army that invaded during the famous battle of the five kingdoms several years ago.

"Who could this be?" asked Finn. "We have no enemies on our island, and we are at peace with all the kingdoms. We defeated Odora several years ago. How could this large of an army sneak up on us in the middle of the night without our defenses seeing them coming?"

Sara said nothing to Finn, but she was very nervous. She could tell by the size of this army that Dunbar would be overwhelmed if they breached the moats and entered the castle. What she did know was this: if Andrew didn't return with reinforcements very soon, Dunbar would fall.

Sara whispered, "Where are you, my love? Dunbar needs you!"

Two

Faith

Three years before the dreaded night invasion, a slow, lazy Sunday afternoon was occurring in Dunbar for the royal family. Andrew, Sara, and their children were having a picnic outside the castle.

"Father, will you please play with us?" asked Karl II. Karl was named after his maternal grandfather, a kind, brave, and loyal man. The whole family loved and respected him.

"Yesses!" Andrew ran toward his children with open arms.

The children ran screaming in opposite directions as Andrew chased them around. Sara was smiling as she watched her husband enthusiastically play with the children. While the family was having fun, two horses were riding at high speeds toward them. As they got nearer, the guards jumped into formation and encircled the royal family. Andrew relaxed when he noticed it was the priest Eamon and a guard with him.

"Andrew, can I have a word with you?" Eamon requested as he dismounted from his black horse. Eamon had perspiration slowly dripping down his forehead, and he looked nervous.

"Yes, Eamon, let's take a walk and discuss what is troubling you," Andrew answered.

"My King, it is your uncle Collin. He has become ill. He has kept it from you because he does not want to burden you, but his condition has grown worse," Eamon explained.

"Wait, what do you mean he is getting worse? I've noticed that he has had a persistent cough and has been tired a lot, but I haven't noticed anything else," Andrew replied.

"Again, my lord, Collin is a dutiful servant of yours and he didn't want to alarm you, so he has kept the worst from you. His cough is getting worse, he has chest discomfort, and most troubling of all is now he is coughing up blood. He doesn't eat much and is very tired. He has kept this from you and the kingdom, but I'm afraid he cannot any longer. I am worried about him and the time he works, it is making him even more fatigued," Eamon explained. As Eamon was talking, Andrew noticed the concern etched across his face. Andrew knew how much Eamon cared for his mentor Collin, and as nephew to Collin, it made the king even more appreciative of this young priest.

"I will gather my family and head back to the castle so I can talk with him. Thank you, Eamon, for letting me know. I know how much he means to you and all the priesthood in the kingdom."

"My lord," Eamon replied, "Collin has only made one request. When you come to see him, he has indicated that he'd like you to bring Sara with you. He wants to speak to both of you at the same time."

"Of course, anything he requested shall be granted," Andrew said.

Eamon left with the guard to rush back to the castle and let Collin know that the king and queen would be visiting soon. Andrew quickly and quietly told Sara the news, and at once, they gathered their things and left.

As Andrew and Sara walked toward Collin's quarters later that day, Andrew made eye contact with his wife. Sara grabbed Andrew's hand and said, "My love, I know how much Collin means to you and I also know he is the last of your kin, so just know that you can confide in me any feelings you are having."

"Thank you, my love, I am okay," Andrew replied.

Andrew pushed open the doors and glanced at his uncle Collin lying in his bed. The king and queen approached Collin who smiled as he saw them.

"My dear nephew, it is so nice to see you and your lovely wife. I am truly sorry I haven't told you of my advancing illness, but I didn't want to burden a busy man," Collin weakly said.

Andrew and Sara gently grabbed his hands and looked down at the head priest of the kingdom. Andrew looked worried as he saw how weak his uncle was, so Sara spoke first.

"Collin, we love you and would never be angry with you. You have been a loyal uncle and servant to the Dunbarian Kingdom. We both have appreciated your loyalty and hard work to make our kingdom stronger."

Collin smiled and made eye contact with the king and queen. He coughed quietly, and then Sara continued.

"Uncle Collin, Andrew and I have always appreciated you. You are a lovely man who has always been a servant of God. Your faith is so inspiring to us. I have always wanted to know, how have you been able to keep such strong faith in God?" Sara asked. Collin smiled as Sara spoke and gave a gentle laugh.

"Oh, lovely Sara, I am so proud of your gracious spirit and love of God. I have unfortunately not always been so faithful," Collin said.

"I have a hard time believing that, Uncle," Andrew replied.

"Now that my time grows shorter, let me tell you a story, a true story that took place long ago in the Dunbar Kingdom. Many, many years ago when I was a young boy, your father, your uncle Duncan, and I were playing outside on a warm spring day. Our cousin, Mack, approached us as we were playing."

"Hey, you three dolts up for a challenge today? My father told me of a Black Hills village not far from our boundaries. Who has the courage to go with me to touch a Black Hills home today?" Mack asked.

"Ah, you are just telling another one of your false tales," Duncan replied.

"And you are chicken! What about you other two cowards? Do you have the guts to go with me?" Mack asked.

James and I looked at each other with doubt, but we didn't want to be called chickens.

"Ok, Mack, we will go with you just to prove you are lying once again," Duncan boldly replied.

The four of us boys ventured out to the south on this warm morning. We walked and walked for what seemed like days, but soon we were nearing the Black Hills village Mack had spoken of.

"See, I told you I was telling the truth! My father never lies. He says this village is called Magadan," Mack boasted.

I looked at my cousin with disgust. I had grown tired of Mack's tall tales and stories. I wanted to embarrass our young cousin who was always trying to show us up.

"So, Mack, now that we are here, why don't you prove how tough you are and touch the outside of that home right over there," I said as I pointed to a small, dirty-looking hut about thirty feet away from us.

Duncan and James both looked at Mack and emphatically told him no. Mack looked nervous but didn't want to look like a coward.

"So, who is the chicken now, Mack?" I asked.

Mack looked around at us and our surroundings. He was sweating but investigated my eyes.

"Fine, I will do it. I will touch the wall of that hut and hurry back to you," Mack said nervously.

It was late afternoon, and the sun was getting lower. Mack looked around to make sure there wasn't anyone around and then crawled out from the forest on his belly and got closer and closer to the hut. There were no people outside, but we could hear voices inside the hut. As Mack got closer, the three of us were watching anxiously. Mack looked back at us as he got right next to the hut. He smiled as he tapped the hut with his index finger and then started to turn around on his stomach so he could head back to us. At that moment, a Black Hills couple walked out of their hut and in the direction of Mack.

"Hey, who are you?" screamed the ugly-looking man with long, greasy black hair. He and his wife ran toward Mack who was sprinting toward us at this point. They caught up with Mack and grabbed him by his collar. The overwhelming fear on his face as he looked desperately toward us was terrifying.

"NO, NO, leave me alone!" Mack screamed.

James, Duncan, and I were all petrified as we watched our cousin being dragged toward the hut and away from us. The evil-looking man yelled at his wife, "Look around the area to see if there are other trespassers!" The three of us were nervously inching our way deeper into the forest as the woman frantically looked all around. We looked at each other with terror. The Black Hills man interrogated

Mack while his wife focused on finding any other intruders lurking around.

"I told you, boy, who are you? What are you doing here? Are there other spies around?" the intimidating man yelled.

Mack was so scared he couldn't utter a reply.

"If you don't speak, boy, I will gut you like a pig!"

Mack was petrified with fear and was crying uncontrollably. As the man looked around wildly, he pulled out his long knife and ended Mack's life. Mack's eyes were staring right at me and then closed. We all put our hands on our mouths so we wouldn't say anything, and tears streamed down my face.

"Sasha, help me tie him up to the wall. It's getting dark soon, we need to warn the village that we have spies around. In the morning, we will make a thorough inspection of the forest."

As the Black Hills couple walked away toward the small village, we looked at each other, all in shock at what we had just witnessed. We were crying softly and shaking. I looked around at my kin and quietly got the courage to speak.

"This is my fault; I should have never told Mack to do that. I want you two to go back to Dunbar. I am going to stay here. When it's safe I'm going to untie his body and take Mack home."

"What?!" said Duncan. "You can't do that, it's too dangerous. We must not separate."

"No, I can't risk you two getting hurt. I can do this Duncan. I will do this! Go, go now. I promise you I will return with his body. NOW go!"

Duncan and James were unsure of what to do, but my determination convinced them that they wouldn't be able to talk me out of it. I grabbed both of my brothers' faces.

"I promise to God above, I will not let you down. I will bring Mack home, don't doubt me. Now go and be careful."

The two princes left me and walked off into the darkness of the night. I looked around and felt all alone. I bowed my head and prayed to God as tears streamed down my face.

"God, please help me. I am truly sorry for what has happened to Mack. It is all my fault! Please help me bring Mack's body back to Dunbar and his family. I swear to you that if you help me do this, I will never doubt you again. I will be your servant and live faithfully for each day of my life. Please, God, show me the way."

I waited for about twenty minutes. I didn't see or hear anything on this dark night. I gathered my courage and crawled to the hut. Quietly as possible, I cut down my dead cousin's arms and legs from the wall of the hut.

"Please, God, give me the strength of Sampson and the courage of Daniel."

I dragged Mack's body to the woods and made a quick look around. I used all my strength and put Mack's lifeless body on my back. I looked ahead of me and took one step forward.

The next day there was a manhunt in Dunbar orchestrated by King James I. When his boys didn't come home the previous night, he assembled his royal guards and army in the war room. There were ten different calvary units dispersed in various directions. In the late afternoon, James and Duncan were found by one of the teams. When James I heard from his boys what had happened, he was gravely concerned for me. When a storm came rumbling in, he had to call off the hunt. The next morning, after a beautiful sunrise, the king led his men out of their camp toward the direction of where I could be. As the king mounted his horse, one of the guards screamed.

"My king, look ahead!" yelled the guard as he pointed in my direction.

As the morning light blinded the king, he put his hand in front of his face. Up ahead he could see me grimacing as I emerged from the forest. I took a slow step and braced myself, and then after a long pause, I took another slow step ahead. My clothes were wet, ripped, and soaked with blood. My hair was disheveled and matted to my head, and the king was shocked to see his nephew's body on my back.

"Men, that's Collin, let's go!" screamed the king. The men galloped hard toward me.

Collin looked up at his nephew, Andrew, and a tear slowly trickled down his face. He grabbed Andrew and Sara's hands.

"From that day forward, I renounced sin. I told myself and God that I would follow him until the ends of the earth. I never wanted to feel shame like I did over what happened to Mack. Every day I get up and ask God for strength so I can live a life dedicated to him."

Andrew and Sara were stunned when they heard this story. They had never heard this before. Sara looked down at Collin and squeezed his hand. She smiled as she said, "I respect you even more than before you told us this story. We will do everything we can to make your time here on Earth as comfortable as possible. Please let us learn from your guidance and wisdom. We love you, dear Uncle!"

THREE

The Enemy

℘wo years before the nighttime attack on the
Dunbarian castle, a long, dangerous journey was
underway. This journey would have enormous consequences for Dunbar and the entire island. A man named
Pavel was climbing an unknown mountain in a foreign
land. The temperature was growing cooler as he climbed
the rocky ledges of this dry mountain. Pavel knew from his
contacts that these mountains held dangerous animals that
could harm him. Large cats at the base of the mountain
called lyons roamed in packs. Further up the mountain the
threat of mountain wolves and leopards persisted. From
what Pavel was told, the leopards were the most dangerous
due to their stealth and ability to blend into their environment. Pavel nervously looked around as he traveled up a
dirt path that was unmarked. Any sound made him almost
jump to attention, and the setting of the sun worried him.
He didn't want to be alone in the dark in this foreign land.

"I hope I find my way to the castle soon; I don't like
being out in the open as the sun sets," Pavel whispered to
himself. Up ahead, he thought he could see something in
the distance. As he moved another twenty feet, two guards
jumped out from crevices in the side of the path he was
walking on. These guards wore turquoise uniforms and
held long, curved swords in their hands.

"Halt! Don't move any closer!" one of the guards fiercely stated.

Pavel was anxious. Did these two guards know that their king was expecting him?

"We have been keeping an eye on you for the past several hours. We were told to watch you to see if you could make it up the mountain. Now that you've proven your endurance, we will escort you the rest of the way," said the shorter of the two guards.

The threesome walked slowly along the dirt path, encountering other guards along the way. As they moved around a curve, Pavel could see the beautiful castle up ahead. It had tan-colored stone with a huge wall built around it that separated it from its moat. The path they were walking on started to get wider and was edged by huge trees that looked very unusual to him.

"What type of trees are these?" Pavel asked.

"They are called palm trees," the guard replied.

These large trees were at least fifty feet tall with beautiful, waxy leaves that were a new sight for Pavel. As the three neared the outer wall, Pavel could see all the archers located at the top of the wall. A huge door started to swing open slowly, and a man wearing a turquoise cloak with an unusual-looking hat came toward Pavel. He was flanked by two menacing-looking guards. As the man approached, Pavel could see many battle scars etched into his leathered face. He had light-green eyes and a black beard speckled with gray groomed very neatly. He was obviously a man of importance in this land.

"Agh, it is nice to finally see you, young Pavel. We have been awaiting your arrival to our beloved land. I take it your journey was uneventful," he said with a low, gravelly voice.

"Yes, uneventful," Pavel nervously replied.

"I am Aadin (he bowed to Pavel as he identified himself), the king's courtier. I will lead you to the king's throne room where King Thoran is patiently awaiting you."

Pavel nodded toward Aadin in approval. There was no talking as they moved past the outer wall and toward the dry moat surrounding this wondrous castle. The dry castle moat was embedded with sharp spikes sticking out of its crusty bottom level. A large lyon with a hairy face looked up at Pavel and growled menacingly. Luckily it was at the bottom of the moat, which Pavel estimated to be fifty feet below. A huge gate was opened, and a tall door swung down from the base of the castle. As they approached the opening, several guards stood in front of their path.

"We must pat down the foreigner," a tall, lanky guard said.

The guards very roughly moved their hands up and down Pavel's body as they were searching for any weapons. Finding none, they escorted the group through the castle.

"As you can see, the king's castle is beyond anything you've ever seen on your island, young Pavel," Aadin quietly uttered.

"Yes, it is very magnificent," Pavel replied.

As they finally reached the king's throne room, there were two creamed-colored doors standing at least fifty feet in the air. Two guards stood at the opposite ends of the doors, both holding on to small, green crocodiles with a leash. The crocodiles hissed and growled as Pavel moved past them. As Pavel walked into the throne room, his eyes could barely take in the extravagance of it all. There were large, brown fans hanging from the ceiling, pushing air comfortably around in this arid environment. Huge, beautiful sculptures were placed strategically around the room. Artwork hung on the walls and servants were playing instruments with soft music. A fountain in the middle of the room displayed the statue of a young, beautiful woman with water slowly pouring through her fingers. At the back of the huge room was an elevated staircase holding an immense throne. The throne had emeralds, sapphires, and other jewels inserted into it. The throne itself was made of gold and it glistened in the sunlight. A handsome man wearing a tall crown stood up as Pavel came closer.

"WE HAVE BEEN PATIENTLY WAITING FOR YOU, PAVEL. IT IS SO NICE YOU ARE FINALLY HERE!" the king blared. Two beautiful spotted leopard cats (chained to the throne) sprang up as the king spoke. They looked at Pavel and growled angrily toward him, which made him start to sweat.

Pavel looked up at the young king and was unable to speak. The sights, sounds, and smells of what he was witnessing were overwhelming.

"I see you are shy, prince of the Black Hills. I understand how my kingdom's extravagance is overwhelming to strangers. You are witnessing the most marvelous kingdom in the world. Come, take a walk with me and we can have a conversation about your visit," the king said.

As the king walked down his throne's steps toward Pavel, the guards moved in closer to Pavel to let him know they were ready at any moment to defend their king if Pavel had any ill intentions. The king reached the bottom of the stairs and Pavel bowed in obedience. As Pavel stood up straight, he noticed he was a few inches taller than the king.

"I, as you already know, am King Thoran. My father, Asiff, was King of the Odoran Kingdom for over twenty years until he was struck down at the battle of Dunbar. The Kingdom of Odora is the grandest in the world. We have the most wonderful land that produces wheat and other grains to feed our obedient people. Lemon, orange, date, and fig trees adorn our cool lakes intermixed with fields of sheep and goats grazing in the hot sun. The castle you are walking in was built by my great-grandfather and is, as you can see, the most advanced castle in the world. Our army has legions and legions of men ready to defend our ancient kingdom at a whim. Our navy spreads out throughout the waters of this world and plunders weaker kingdoms of their treasures. We are the most powerful, advanced kingdom in the world."

King Thoran, Pavel, and Aadin walked into a large, open-roofed room with a huge, crystal-clear pool. Surrounding the pool were citrus fruit trees and small palm trees. Young, olive-skinned women were fanning a woman sitting by the pool.

"That, my friend, is my wife. Her name is Aleah, which means exalted one. She is the most beautiful woman in the world," Thoran boasted.

Pavel smiled in agreement for she was incredibly attractive, but he was unsure of how to respond to the boastful king. He knew anything he said may be misinterpreted by these sly people.

"Let's get down to business, shall we, young Pavel," Thoran said. "We reached out to you because we have spies on your island. Our spies indicated that you have been actively leading a quiet uprising against Sergio who is the King of the Black Hills, but you don't have many numbers, maybe ten families?"

Pavel was impressed with the king's knowledge and replied, "Yes, we have nearly ten families who along with me believe that our king has betrayed our heritage. It is disgusting to know that the Black Hills have an alliance with that despicable Dunbar Kingdom after everything they've done against us," Pavel angrily said before spitting on the ground. "I swore an allegiance to my uncle Igor, the true King of the Black Hills. He must have been hypnotized with Dunbarian sorcery the day he relented to those frauds Andrew and Duncan. There is no way he would have freely given in to their persuasion unless he was hypnotized. He's dead and our so-called King Sergio is a farce who is turning our once proud kingdom into a laughingstock amongst the islanders. I will do whatever it takes to seek revenge on Dunbar and the other kingdoms so the true Black Hills Kingdom rules again!"

Thoran laughed maniacally. "My friend, I love the hatred you show for your enemies. I LOATH these same miserable people! Andrew and these other "leaders" on your island killed my father, the great Asiff. They embarrassed our people and brought shame to my family. As soon as our army came home, I begged my older brother Ferman to rally our troops and send them back to kill EVERYONE on that island, but he refused. He was the new king and said it would be better for our kingdom if we just moved on. I told him that our enemies on the continent would hear of our defeat and then we would be vulnerable to their attack. Again, he denied my request, so I did what needed to be done to seek revenge for our father. I convinced my mother that for the better of Odora, I must execute my brother and be the exulted king. After becoming king, I knew I would develop a plan to invade their island and destroy Dunbar."

"You executed your own brother?" Pavel replied.

"Yes, he was a barrier to Odora's best interest. Do you want to know how I did it?" Thoran asked.

Pavel shook his head.

"I took him to our dungeon and put him in the pit, which is thirty feet deep. It is a cave in the middle of the dungeon room. In it, there are four gates leading to the outside. When placed in the pit, the prisoner has a choice; lyon, bear, crocodile, or leopard. Whichever he chooses will come out of one of the gates." Thoran laughed.

Pavel was truly appalled at the evilness of the Odoran King, but he needed him to seek revenge on Andrew.

"I HATE Andrew, I HATE the five kingdoms on your island, and I HATED my brother for being so weak. I will get my revenge and the punishment they will receive will be ten times worse than what Ferman received! Our plan is almost complete. Be patient, young Pavel, our time is almost here. Once the preparations are complete, my people will alert you and we will make our move. Go, get your small army prepared for what they will need to do. We will rule the island together after we destroy the four false kingdoms led by Andrew. Make sure your spies in the other kingdom make their preparations. When we are all ready, we will strike like a snake, and they won't know what has hit them!" Thoran growled.

"Thank you, oh mighty Thoran, I promise you I will not falter in this task. We will both have our revenge and rule the island forever!" Pavel said as he smiled widely.

Four

The Missing Kingdom

ne year before the horrible nighttime attack on the Dunbar castle, Andrew and Sara were venturing into the great Blue Forest to drink from the green emerald. After Andrew's uncle Duncan had died, he told Sara about the emerald and the angel Joseph. He explained that only two could take the journey to the forest and drink from the emerald. He explained that Duncan and he had ventured several times to the emerald and had conversed with the angel Joseph. Sara was at first doubtful of her husband's tale, but she had always trusted him to be honest and forthright, so she agreed to go with him.

"My darling, are we almost there?" Sara asked.

"Yes, my dear, it is up ahead a few minutes," Andrew replied.

The two had been wandering along in the forest on this cool spring morning. Sara was unaccustomed to this forest for she had only ventured into it a few times. This jaunt with her husband was a pleasant trip.

"How do you think the children are doing without us?" Sara asked.

"Oh, I think they are all doing fine. I would guess that they are happy to have a day away from their parents. You know how children are," Andrew replied.

With it being early spring the vegetation hadn't reached its full potential yet, but Sara was delighted to see alliums, anemones, bluebells, and daffodils scattered about.

"There it is." Andrew pointed to an outgrowth of trees clustered together.

Sara looked at the huge clump of trees and wondered how they were going to penetrate them. Sara watched her husband from a distance and then followed him through the opening Andrew had cleared.

"My love, how did you know where that opening was?" Sara asked.

"I told you, dear lassie, that I have ventured here several times with Duncan. I could find this blindfolded, if need be," Andrew replied.

Andrew reached into the shallow stream of water and pulled out a large green emerald. As soon as Andrew pulled out the emerald, a white light shown, and the angel Joseph appeared. Sara was stunned even though Andrew had told her what was to come.

"King Andrew, it is nice to see you again," Joseph uttered. "Please, Queen Sara, come forward and see me. Don't be afraid, I am an angel of the Lord."

"Yes, Joseph, I hear you," Sara replied as she stepped forward.

"God has looked favorably on you, young queen. He sees in your soul that you are faithful and pure. You are a truly wonderful example to your people. Continue putting all your faith in the Lord and he will bless you," Joseph said.

Joseph then looked at the two of them and said, "God has watched your kingdom and is pleased. He is happy with how the two of you have proclaimed his name and led your island toward more prosperity. You have done well, and God has been favorable toward your kingdom. But I am here today to caution you. There is a great storm brewing. Another invader is approaching, one that will bring destruction and chaos. There is still time to thwart this invasion, but you MUST unite the entire island by righting a wrong that was done many, many years ago. Your island isn't truly united, Andrew, not yet, for there is still something missing. Go to the top of Mount Nevis. There you will find the Tree of Kings, which will give you answers. Go, and God be with you always!"

Sara and Andrew watched as Joseph disappeared. Both were perplexed with Joseph's pronouncement but knew to trust in it completely.

"My love, do you know what Joseph meant by saying the island isn't united completely? All five kingdoms have been unified," Sara said.

"No, my queen, I do not. But I do know this, Joseph has always been true to his word. Every word he has spoken has come true and our kingdom has truly been blessed when we follow God's word. We must believe in him and do as he says," Andrew replied.

A week later, to the surprise of the king's court, Andrew and Sara were off again on an adventure by themselves. The secrecy of their trip was perplexing to many, but Andrew had promised them that it was necessary for the kingdoms' prosperity.

The Tree of Kings is an ancient, Birnam Oak tree that legend says was where the kings all met to divide the island into their perspective kingdoms over a millennium ago. The tree sits atop the rocky cliffs of Mount Nevis, the most elevated place on the island. It was a tough climb to the top of the mountain for the terrain was rocky and steep with several dangerous animal species located in the area. The only poisonous snake on the island, the hognose, was known to exist in the crevices of the rocky cliffs. There were occasional sightings of black bears and coal cats as well.

At the top of the mountain was a flock of mountain sheep with enormous, aggressive rams living amongst them. Only the stealthiest coal cat could take on one of these hardy, bellicose animals. Andrew knew this was going to be a dangerous climb and was a little nervous at the thought of bringing his wife into this situation.

"My darling, we are entering a dangerous area. Please follow my lead so we both come back unscathed," Andrew said.

"Yes, dear, I will be careful. Have you ever scaled this mountain before?" asked the queen.

"Not since I was a boy, and my father was very protective as we did. It is a dangerous climb. Keep an eye out when you reach for a place to set your hands, snakes like crawling out to sunbathe on the outgrowths. Also, be aware of any carnivores that roam through this area. When I was a boy, we saw a bear family meandering around," Andrew replied.

The two royals were sweating as they made the hard climb up the rocky incline. The sun had come out, and it was the warmest day yet this spring. Sara was breathing heavily, and Andrew was sweating a great deal.

As Sara reached up to pull herself to the next level, she asked, "How much farther?"

Andrew, breathing hard, replied, "Just one more incline and we're there."

As Andrew helped push Sara up to the top peak, he could hear the unmistakable bleating of sheep.

Andrew pulled himself up to join his wife and looked up at their surroundings. There was mountain scrub scattered throughout the area. A few mountain figs and pear trees were also there. As Andrew looked out at the horizon, he saw the wonderful Tree of Kings. It was located over one hundred feet away in front of the dry, rocky mountainside.

The tree was easily the largest at the top of this mountain and its girth was impressive. It had a wide base that was probably fifteen feet wide with six thick branches that spread out in opposite directions from each other. Each branch was enormous and ran parallel to the ground but then shot up toward the sky. The bark was brittle, and each branch had a small number of dry leaves colored an unattractive brown.

Andrew looked ahead toward the tree then looked at his wife. "Sara, there is the tree we are looking for. Do you see it?"

"Yes, I do, it is very distinctive," Sara replied.

"Sara, be cautious. I heard the bleating of wild mountain sheep as we scaled the cliffs, which means rams may be present too. These animals have been known to kill men. Please walk behind me and be careful."

The two of them moved slowly as they walked amongst the dry, mountain scrub and fruit trees. As they moved into an opening, they saw the sheep grazing out in an open area. As soon as the sheep saw them, they bleated loudly and formed a circle around the ewes and lambkin. Enormous rams grunted and snorted as they looked nervously at the intruders on their territory.

Andrew whispered to his wife, "Walk slowly behind me." Andrew slowed his pace, but as soon as he got within ten feet of them, three large rams charged at him. Andrew's quick reflexes were impressive, but two black-coated rams knocked him off his feet and pinned him down on the ground with their thick horns. Andrew was yelling as he tried pushing up against their combined strength.

"Sara, move back. I'm going to need to kill them with my cutlass."

The rams were pushing Andrew's body into the dirt and one of the ram's horns was thrusting into his ribs.

Sara was scared for her husband, and she knew she needed to move quickly for her own protection, or she would suffer the same fate. But her feet felt as if they couldn't move. She looked up and saw the alpha ram of the herd looking straight at her. This ram was around a hundred pounds with shaggy light-blue hair covering its entire body. It had enormous horns and was very intimidating. It was snorting into the air to warn her to back off. It charged several times, finally stopping just short of Sara, who was petrified with fear.

Sara whispered a quick prayer and composed herself. She looked at her husband who was in grave danger and then back at the dominant ram. As she looked into the ram's eyes, she started singing an ancient hymn she had loved as a child and sang many times to her own children:

In days of old when the world was young,
God whispered words, and the song was sung.
Mountains rose and rivers flowed,
In every tree, His blessings glowed.

Oh, the beauty of the earth, the sky so wide,
In every creature, His love abides.
From the mighty oak to the smallest bee,
God's hand has crafted all we see.

In forests deep and oceans grand,
He painted wonders with His hand.
The eagle's flight, the dolphin's play,
Each one cherished in its own way.

Oh, the beauty of the earth, the sky so wide,
In every creature, His love abides.
From the mighty oak to the smallest bee,
God's hand has crafted all we see.

The wolf's howl, the lyon's roar,
The whispering winds on every shore.
In every leaf and every stone,
His glory shines, we are never alone.

In every heart and every soul,
He placed a spark, made us whole.
No creature small, no being slight,
In His grand design, we are all light.

Oh, the beauty of the earth, the sky so wide,
In every creature, His love abides.
From the mighty oak to the smallest bee,
God's hand has crafted all we see.

So sing the song of ancient days,
Of God's great love and endless praise.
In nature's arms, we find our place,
Each one worthy, touched by grace.

Sara's voice was as sweet as the purest honey, and it mesmerized the flock of sheep. As soon as Sara finished singing, she locked eyes with the dominant ram. She got down on her knees and bowed to the great ram. She looked up at him, and as if they were communicating through thoughts, the dominant ram snorted. The two black-coated rams relaxed and let Andrew stand. Then the flock parted and moved back. Sara walked over to Andrew and reached for his hand. As the two held hands they walked slowly between the sheep. They could hear the breathing of the sheep, but they looked straight ahead toward the Tree of Kings as they walked.

After they moved away from them a safe distance Andrew asked, "My love, what just happened? How did you know to do that?"

"I asked God for his wisdom, and he told me to use my voice to calm them."

"I am so glad you used your wits. I don't know if I could have gotten out of that situation with my life. God knows how beautiful your voice is my love. It can calm the wildest storm at sea."

Sara blushed and thanked her husband. They approached the tree and stood looking up at its huge branches splaying out. The branches began a few feet above the ground, strong and solid, before rising high into the air.

"Well, what now?" Sara asked.

"Let's take a closer look," Andrew said. They both investigated the branches and the base of the tree.

"Oh, my goodness, Andrew. There is something carved into this branch. Come look!"

As Andrew approached, he could see the outline of words sketched on the base of one of the large branches. It said Woodendale and had its royal symbol drawn next to it. It was undeniably carved with some sort of knife many, many years ago. Andrew ran to another large branch and found the word Lancot carved with its royal symbol next to it.

"Sara, each of these branches has the name of a kingdom written down with its symbol next to it."

"But Andrew, there are six branches and there are only five kingdoms on the island," Sara retorted.

"Well, let's find them all and see."

The two royals found Dunbar on another branch, and then the Black Hills. They next found Watertown and ran toward the last of the six big branches. As they got to the huge branch and looked down at its base, they saw something they didn't recognize. On this large branch was the word Northlanders. Next to it was a symbol of a long-sleeved surcoat with a cross in the middle of it.

Andrew and Sara looked at each other in disbelief. Both doubted what they were seeing but knew from Joseph's message that this must be the missing piece of information they needed.

"We must get back to the castle and figure out what this means. Is there anyone who would have knowledge of this kingdom?" Sara asked. Andrew looked at his wife and said, "We must see Collin at once!"

When the two of them reached the castle, they brushed aside the welcoming party. They tried hiding their anxiousness and inquired about Collin.

"My king, Collin is resting in his room at this moment. He has been sleeping most of the day," acting high priest Eamon said.

"I need to see him at once, please wake him."

The king's uncle, Collin, had been the high priest of the kingdom since before Andrew was a little boy. He was a kind, gentle, humble man who had led the people of Dunbar in religious matters for generations. However, the royal family had watched his health decline over the last several years, and Collin hadn't left his room in months.

Andrew and Sara walked into the room and looked down on Collin who was sitting in the middle of his bed with covers tucked up to his chin. He had visibly shrunk in stature and his face was sunken in. His breathing was labored but when he saw his nephew and beautiful wife, he smiled.

"It is so nice to see two of my favorite people in the world. How are you, my nephew?"

"I am well, Uncle. How are you?" Andrew replied.

"Well, I'd be lying if I said good. Each new day on Earth is a blessing," Collin whispered.

Collin could see the consternation in the king's eyes and said, "What is it nephew, I can see you are troubled."

"Uncle, we have come to see you for an answer. Do you know if there ever was another kingdom on this island? A sixth kingdom?"

Collin looked surprised at Andrew's question and closed his eyes for a second. Then he looked up at his nephew.

"I should've mentioned this to you a long time ago. Especially since I don't have much time left, and I may be the only one who still knows the truth. This kingdom you mention was called the Northlanders. Their warriors wore a white long-sleeved surcoat with a large red cross down the middle. They were located between Woodendale and our kingdom. They were a peaceful trading ally of ours. Over five hundred years ago, there was a falling out between their king and ours. A dispute over an incident that happened between a hunting party of the Black Hills led by their King Dmitriy and our protector Bruce. A heated conversation occurred when their King Gunner accused Bruce's hunting party of killing Dmitriy's men without necessity. Our king at the time, Liam, convinced the Woodendale Kingdom to join with us and banish the Northlanders. We pushed them off their lands, and they were forced to abandon the island. It was a grave injustice, for Liam later realized that the Black Hills hunting party that day were not the aggressors. His brother Bruce admitted it didn't need to turn to violence, but it was too late, the Northlanders were already gone. They abandoned their castle and lands and headed north into the ocean. They took over an almost uninhabited island that we all know to be Ice Island of the North. These Northlanders as we know today have the farthest north and westerly trading post in the ocean. The Watertown Kingdom trades with them regularly. Nobody on this island truly knows of this tale except me and the King of Woodendale, Elaran. It was passed down to him from his father, the late King Bailey. It was a travesty to the Northlanders and a stain on our kingdom. All of Dunbar's kings since Liam have known of this tale and now my nephew, you do too."

Andrew was stunned, for his father had never told him of this. He looked at Sara in disbelief and looked back at his loyal uncle.

"Uncle, is there anything written down about this or is it just an oral tale?" Andrew asked.

"Andrew, pull away the curtains on the east wall of my room," said Collin. Andrew and Sara did as Collin said and pulled the long, green curtain back. Behind it was a huge tapestry with a beautiful red background. In the middle of the tapestry was the picture of six kings all looking at each other in a circle smiling. Each was a king of the island, for Andrew could tell by their colors and uniforms which king was which. He looked for a very long time at the Dunbarian King and admired his attributes. Then, for the first time, he saw what a King of Northland looked like. A tall, blond-haired man with a golden crown wearing a white surcoat with a large red cross in the middle of it. He was a very distinguished-looking king and Andrew felt a sense of melancholy looking at this tapestry knowing that the bond between the kingdoms was broken by his own family.

"Uncle, do we know when this tapestry was made?" Andrew asked.

"No, nephew, we don't. It was made before the great disruption and banishment of the Northlanders. But what this tapestry proves is there was an alliance between all the kingdoms. There is also a book on the top shelf of my dresser drawer. It has the complete history of the six kingdoms on the island, including the forced removal of the Northlanders. It is now yours, please read it to get more information. Now, my king, I have a question for you, why are you asking me about the Northlanders?"

Andrew locked eyes with Sara, and he was struggling to come up with an answer when Sara responded.

"Beloved uncle, we have come across a message that it is dire for us to reconcile with this sixth kingdom. We can't say how we got this message, but please trust us," Sara replied.

Collin pondered what Sara said and spoke very slowly, "My lovely nephew and his beautiful wife, please know this, I trust you more than anyone in this world. The two of you have reunited the Black Hills with the other kingdoms, and you've brought peace and prosperity to this island. I don't need to know how you got this message; I believe in you two and God believes in the two of you. Do what you must."

Andrew and Sara both kissed Collin on the cheek and left his room. They knew at that moment that there was no time to waste; they must find a way to reach Ice Island and ask their king for forgiveness before it was too late. If the angel Joseph was correct, the survival of all the kingdoms depended on this voyage.

"Sara, I will read this book tonight. Once I have more knowledge of this forgotten kingdom, I will bring a small battalion of men with me to Watertown. I know I can convince King Addison to join me on the trip to Ice Island. Watertown has a trade alliance with this kingdom, and I'll need his help. Now, Sara, you will need to stay here and lead our kingdom. I have the utmost faith in your ability. I don't know how long this journey will take me, but the people of our kingdom trust you completely. I am confident that I will be back before this invader Joseph was cautioning us about arrives."

A week later Sara watched as her husband left with his battalion of men. Nobody in the kingdom except Sara knew of his true destination, and Sara hoped she would be up to the task of protecting the kingdom.

As Andrew looked back one more time at Sara, she whispered to herself, "May God watch over you and our kingdom."

Five

The Fury

Nine months before the night of the invasion, there happened to be a beautiful, warm day in the Dunbar Kingdom. While walking around the castle you could smell and taste the aroma of the surrounding flora. A light breeze and sun-filled sky lifted even the grouchiest of residents' spirits. Sara was really missing Andrew, having not heard from him for three months. As she opened the curtains, she smiled. Looking down at children playing in the morning sun and families moving about through their morning chores, she felt invigorated.

"Oh, Andrew, I hope you are doing well today. It is such a beautiful day; I wish we could spend the day together riding our horses through the countryside. Please be careful, my love," Sara whispered out loud to herself.

After dressing and washing up, Sara went to morning Mass. She then had some breakfast and went to get her morning update from Timothy, second in command for the royal guard.

"Good morning, my queen, what a beautiful day it is," Timothy said.

"Yes, Timothy, it is certainly a gorgeous day. God couldn't make a better one, could he?" Sara asked.

"No, this is as pleasant as it gets, my queen. Well, I don't have much information on this day, but there is one thing that needs your attention. One of the largest sheep-herders in the kingdom is here to speak with you. He has had a terrible situation occur with his flock."

The queen and Timothy walked into the royal throne room and took a seat. In walked a tall, thin man with a long white beard. He approached the queen very slowly. He had piercing blue eyes and wore a modest shepherd's cloak over his worn-out pants. He looked very tense as he approached the queen.

"Can I make a request to the queen?" the man asked Timothy.

"Yes, go right ahead," Timothy replied.

"My queen, I am here today to ask for the kingdom's help in a matter that has affected my family but also the kingdom as a whole. Three days ago, my large flock of sheep wandered off from my two sons. By the time they noticed, the sheep had entered the Blue Forest. It is the law of Dunbar that we need permission to enter the forest from the royalty, so I am here today to ask for this permission. The number of my flock is above five hundred and provides much for the kingdom. I need to get to them immediately before predators do. Thank you, my grace," he stated.

"I am glad you have come to the castle to request this. We know this must be stressful for you to have your sheep unattended to. I will have Timothy organize a squad of soldiers at once to venture into the Blue Forest with you. Hopefully, you will be able to retrieve all your missing flock," Sara said smiling.

"Timothy, can you request Fergus report to the great hall so he can be informed of the situation before he leads this squad into the forest?" Sara said.

"My queen, Fergus is out of the kingdom again with Grigori. Someone else will need to lead this expedition," Timothy replied.

"He's gone again," Sara said in a puzzled manner. "He has been spending a lot of time away from the kingdom with Grigori. I feel like he is never around the castle anymore."

"Yes, I get a strange feeling when I'm around Grigori. There is an evil aura that emanates from him. I don't like the prince spending so much time with him," Timothy added.

"We can discuss that later, Timothy," Sara said.

Timothy nodded to the queen who sighed. She then dismissed the shepherd and decided to change her plans.

"Timothy, with Scott being ill, you will oversee security for the castle. I don't want to take you away from the defenses. Angus and his men are training currently so I don't want to interfere for such a small situation. Why don't I have high royal guard Cameron lead this group of soldiers and I'll go with. I can bring my son Karl along with me."

Timothy took a little time to think of this and then said, "Cameron is ready for this task, and I agree having your son gain this experience will be good for him. May God bless you, my lady, and safe travels."

Early the next morning the queen's royal carriage left the Dunbarian castle and headed toward the Blue Forest. The journey was uneventful. Sara spent her time informing Karl about the history of the kingdom and the peculiar forest they were entering. The small traveling party met the shepherd and his four sons. They had two large sheepdogs with them.

"We have tracked our sheep to this spot where they entered the forest. We should follow it until we get close to the sheep. My sons can make a call that will bring them to us."

"That sounds like a good plan." Cameron looked at Sara. She nodded in agreement. The next several hours the group ventured farther into the forest. The temperature was warming up and the sounds of the forest were alive. Songbirds, squirrels, raccoons, and other small creatures were moving about and making a lot of racket. The five shepherds were making sheep calls while the dogs were following a trail with their noses. The group heard bleating in the distance and started moving quickly toward the noise. The dogs raced ahead of the group and then out of sight.

Sara, Karl, and Cameron were walking behind the soldiers when out of nowhere a large female coal cat jumped out of some tall vegetation and onto Cameron's back. It bit into him, and he called out in pain. The man and beast rolled onto the ground as the soldiers ran to help Cameron. As the first soldier came upon the cat it released its grip from Cameron and let out a terrifying growl, sending goosebumps down the backs of Sara and all the men. The soldiers formed a phalanx in front of the menacing cat. Sara and Karl rushed toward Cameron to investigate his injuries. As Sara examined his injuries, they heard a scream up ahead where the shepherds were wrangling the sheep. Loud sounds echoed toward the group, as though animals were fighting. The soldiers all turned toward the sounds, and at that moment, the coal cat that attacked Cameron sprang toward the nearest soldier and swiped him across his face. Large bloody scratch marks instantly appeared on his face.

"AGGGGHHHH!" the soldier screamed. The cat ran away from the group into the vegetation. The soldiers broke the phalanx and charged into the vegetation after it.

"NO, don't leave us!" Sara yelled.

Sara and Karl were looking frantically around for something to use for Cameron's wounds when another large, male coal cat came out of the ferns stalking toward them.

"NO, you will not harm us!" Sara screamed at the cat.

Her yelling did nothing to deter the large cat. It looked menacing as it growled in a low, threatening way. Sara stood in front of Karl and brandished her cutlass sword. The cat jumped in the air toward Sara. Right before it landed on her, Karl sprang from behind her and thrust his sword into the cat's underbelly. It let out a death-curdling scream and ran away from them with the sword still hanging from its underbelly. Sara hugged Karl and looked at him with admiration. Just then Cameron screamed in pain. Sara looked behind her and another cat had the back of his head in its mouth. It started dragging him away deeper into the underbrush. The returning soldiers came running back at the sound of Cameron screaming.

"A cat is taking Cameron into the vegetation. You must get him!" Sara shrieked. Two soldiers stayed with the queen and her son as the rest of the soldiers ran toward Cameron.

"Let's run ahead toward the shepherds to check on them," Sara yelled.

The two soldiers put Sara and Karl in between them and ran ahead. As they reached the shepherds, they saw blood all over the forest floor. Two of the sons were hunched over and tending to one of their sheepdogs that had life-ending wounds. The father and other sons were gathering all the sheep into a circle.

"What happened?" Karl asked.

"A cat came out from those sumacs and attacked our two dogs. It injured this one here, which is now dying. The other dog was lured into the forest. We could hear fighting, but it has gone quiet. We are gravely concerned the dog has perished. We need to get these sheep out of this forest as quickly as possible."

"I agree, let's get out of here before more bloodshed happens," Sara responded.

The soldiers led Sara and Karl to the front of the herd of sheep, and they started following the path back to the edge of the forest. In five minutes, time, they came across the rest of the soldiers. Two of them had Cameron positioned on their backs.

"My queen, we need to move out of this forest. Cameron's wounds are life-threatening, and one of our men has gone missing. For your safety, we need to go now!"

"Yes, I believe we should. We can't see where these cats are coming from until they're on us," Sara replied.

The sheep were loudly bleating as the group toiled ahead. As they finally reached the edge of the forest, the sheep quickly sprinted ahead into the open field. The shepherds were counting the sheep as they all sighed in relief to be out of the dangerous forest. As Sara was about to speak the group heard another blood-curdling scream coming from the forest.

"It's the sound of one of the cats," the shepherd said.

"Let's move farther away just to be a little safer," Sara replied.

As they moved deeper into the open field, the sun was setting. The soldiers put Cameron on the ground. His breathing was labored, and all the color had drained from him.

"My queen, please tell my family I love them," Cameron weakly stated.

"Keep your strength, everything will be ok. You will live Cameron," the queen replied.

"No, my time is near, I'm so cold and tired. Please let them know I was brave," Cameron stated.

As he said this, he gasped his last breath. Sara started crying and closed his eyes.

"We must carry his body the rest of the way. Come here and help me," she stated to the soldiers.

They wearily picked him up and headed for home. It was a long, chilly walk back to the carriage. Nobody spoke a word that night; they all were too tired and emotionally drained. The only sounds of that dark night came from the bleating of the sheep who were happy to be found.

Six

Forgiveness

ix months before that dreaded nighttime attack, Andrew was on the Watertown boat headed for Ice Island in the North. Andrew and his son James III were guests on the King of Watertown's boat. Andrew had recently been told a terrible story of how his kingdom had unjustly banished the Northlander Kingdom many years ago, and he was searching for them so he could right this terrible wrong. King Addison and his crew were leading this large vessel toward Ice Island, which was located north and west of the island of five kingdoms. To Andrew's knowledge, only the Watertown Kingdom had ventured this far into the ocean before. The experience of the fishermen and explorers of Watertown was widely known throughout the island, and all five kingdoms relied on the imports they brought in from all over the ocean.

This ship, called a cog, had a flat bottom which made it easier to load and unload cargo. King Addison's crew was made up of the best sailors in his kingdom, each was experienced and tough. They had all sailed for many years and had knowledge of the ocean. Addison had wearily accepted Andrew's request to take him to Ice Island because he felt that all the kings on the island owed Andrew for his leadership in the victorious war against Odora several years ago. When Andrew told him he couldn't tell him why he needed to reach the island, Addison was bewildered but trusted his old friend. The two of them had, over the last several weeks, discussed how things were going on the island and Andrew's future plans. James took this time to listen and learn. He was amazed at how much logical, thoughtful consideration it took to be a ruler of a kingdom.

"Andrew, we have almost arrived at the island. Once we get a little closer, you will see two large statues of soldiers flanking the main village along the coast. You will be impressed with the size of these statues and the detail in their facial structures."

"King Addison, have you ever discussed with the people on Ice Island their heritage?" Andrew asked.

"No, this discussion has never been brought up. Why do you ask?" Addison asked.

"Well, I'm just curious as to who I will be conversing with," Andrew replied.

"The King of Ice Island is named Magnus. He is an inquisitive, logical, compassionate man who has been king for as long as I have had contact with them. The people living on the island are hard-working, honest people who stick to themselves. What is unusual about the island is there are people from various races on it. You will see people with snow-white complexions and others with extremely dark complexions. I don't know the history of why that is so, but I'm sure Magnus can tell us. Oh, look up ahead!" Addison pointed excitedly.

Andrew and James looked at the horizon and saw the largest statues they had ever seen; they must have been over several hundred feet tall. Both statues were of soldiers who looked over the ocean with ominous, stern looks.

"This is the harbor for the city Nuuki, which is the main village along the coast. It is the hub for all the imports and exports of the island. Wait, did you see that ripple in the water? Look ahead about fifty feet, there's something in the water," Addison anxiously stated.

"Yes, there is something in the water. The ripples are huge," Andrew stated.

Addison and Andrew were walking toward the side of the boat when they saw the chief mate and crew running toward the side of the boat. The chief mate's body tensed up as he screamed with all his might, "Ketea! Ketea! There is a huge ketea up ahead, get the weapons, men!"

The crew ran toward the weapons area and grabbed long spears and bows. As they were doing this, Andrew for the first time saw this huge beast rise out of the water. Its head was enormous, almost as big as the boat itself. The color of the ketea was dark gray, and its eye was focused on the boat. The crew was terrified as they braced themselves for the inevitable confrontation that was about to happen.

The crew started heaving spears at the beast, but most missed their mark. The head of the ketea dropped below the water and then disappeared. The men frantically looked all around the sides of the boat when suddenly, a powerful force slammed into the stern. The force was so strong it lifted the boat into the air, and a cracking sound could be heard. Two sailors fell into the water, and others were screaming directions as they chaotically ran around the deck. The ketea swam about one hundred yards ahead before it started turning around. Sailors linked arms as they reached down to pull the fallen men up.

"Men, pull harder! The creature is coming back, hurry!" the chief mate screamed.

The ketea was picking up steam as it roared ahead toward the boat. One sailor was pulled over the side before the men had to break the connection to the other fallen sailor. The ketea again dropped below the surface. Moments later it resurfaced in front of the bow of the boat.

Its mighty jaws were wide open as it crunched down on the wooden pieces. The boat fell forward as the beast held onto the front of the ship. Water was rushing onto the ship, and the keel could be heard cracking under the pressure of the ketea. Several sailors had direct hits with long spears, and the ketea grunted out a horrifying noise as it released its hold. It swam furiously away from the boat.

"Men, we must muster up all our strength when it returns. The ship is going to sink if we don't kill the beast," screamed the chief mate.

Andrew, James, and Addison were in shock as they witnessed this monster take down the ship. Andrew looked over at his terrified son. He then looked at the faces of the sailors scattered throughout the deck and could see the fear in their eyes. He knew they would all sink into the ocean if something wasn't done.

"I will not let my son die on this boat. I WILL NOT! I must do something to save him and these men," Andrew said out loud.

He looked over the side of the boat in the direction of the ketea. The large, gray-colored creature was powering toward the stern side of the boat. He looked around the deck searching for a weapon he could use, and from the corner of his eye, he saw a large harpoon hoisted against the side deck. He darted toward the harpoon with cat-like reflexes and grabbed it by its base. He turned around and rushed to the stern as the ketea was barreling toward it. As he looked on the horizon, his eyes met the ketea's. At that moment, man and beast understood that only one was going to survive this day. As Andrew neared the stern of the boat, he could see it rise out of the water headfirst. Its head was slanted, and its teeth were visible as it soared high above the stern of the boat. Andrew could see the scars and crevices on the side of the ketea's face. Its teeth had seaweed stuck to them and barnacles clung to its side. Andrew was racing toward the monster and leapt up high into the air holding onto the harpoon with his right hand. As he soared through the air, just feet away from this monster, he thrust the harpoon as forcefully as possible. The sharp, steel object shot out of his hand like a cannon and into the soft right eye of the creature. Instantly the animal let out an enormous sound so frightening, the men cowered on the deck. It fell onto the edge of the boat and swayed its head from side to side. Andrew held onto the boat as the ketea slowly slid off the edge and into the water. It submerged deep into the water, leaving the men on the boat to tend to the wounded. The sailors jumped in the air and screamed in excitement as the beast disappeared. Andrew stood up and looked over at Addison and James, who were smiling at this great warrior!

Seven days later Andrew and Addison's small group was entering the great hall of Ice Island. The entire hall was crammed with inhabitants of this northern island. Men and women wore long-sleeved wool tunics with red crosses in the middle of them. The women had long, blond hair that was braided. The men had shaggy, blond hair and were bearded. Many of the people in the room looked different though. They had black skin with black hair and beards. Yet, they, too, were wearing the same cross tunics. As Addison, James, and Andrew approached King Magnus's throne, Andrew for the first time got a good look at Magnus. The king of Ice Island was an incredibly large man with a long, blond beard. He had piercing blue eyes.

Magnus stood up and with a loud, boisterous voice bellowed, "Addison, King of Watertown, it is such an honor to have you finally visit our humble island. You have brought with you Andrew, the ketea slayer! What a great tale your people will tell of your brave battle with the sea beast!"

"King Magnus, I am humbled to be in your great kingdom and to be standing in front of you. Our trading alliance has been beneficial to both of our kingdoms, and I greatly respect you."

"Thank you, my fellow king. I hope your stay has been well. When word reached me that two kings from the southern island wanted a meeting, I was greatly intrigued. Besides Watertown, we have only known of each other through trade. I am very curious as to why the King of Dunbar would like an audience with me, in my own kingdom."

"People of Ice Island, great King Magnus, I am Andrew, the King of Dunbar. I have asked for an audience in your grand hall to right a great wrong. I have only become aware of a situation that occurred many, many years ago on our island, and I am here to ask your kingdom for forgiveness."

"Forgiveness? I don't understand. I think an explanation is in order," Magnus replied.

"Well, as I stated, I have only recently become aware that several hundred years ago, your Kingdom of Ice Island was located on our island. Andrew pulled out the tapestry (the one his uncle Collin gave him) from his satchel and opened it up. Here is a tapestry from our castle that shows all the kingdoms located on our island, Watertown, Black Hills, Dunbar, Woodendale, Lancot, and Northland. Each of these kingdoms were at one time peaceful toward each other and shared in the island's resources. Even the Black Hills were on friendly terms with the rest, but over time there became distrust between them and Woodendale and Dunbar especially. A terrible incident happened in the Blue Forest over five hundred years ago. A hunting party of the Black Hills was wandering through the woods and was confronted by a group of Dunbarian soldiers led by Bruce, the king's brother. The Black Hills men were all killed, and

Bruce told his brother, the king, that it was in self-defense. Somehow, the King of Northland knew that this was not so. He confronted the Kings of Dunbar and Woodendale and implored them to admit this attack wasn't in self-defense. He urged them to make amends with the Black Hills, or the future of the island would be in peril. Grave things would happen if this wasn't fixed. The two Kings of Dunbar and Woodendale got angry and joined forces. Instead of working together to right a wrong, they banished the Northlanders and split their lands between them. The Northlanders left the island for good, never coming back, and searched the seas until they landed here, on Ice Island. Again, I did not know of this event until recently. My uncle, the great priest Collin, gave me a book and told me of this horrible story. Andrew reached into his satchel and pulled out the book. After learning of this horrible piece of our island's history, I have come to this island to beg your forgiveness and ask what our kingdoms can do to make this up to you." Andrew stated as he bowed to Magnus.

"King of Dunbar, are you sincere in what you are saying?" Magnus asked.

"Yes, great king, I have never been more sincere. I feel terrible about what happened to your people. What occurred is a disgrace, and I speak for my kingdom when I say we will do whatever it takes to make up for this horrible event. Oh, mighty King Magnus, I beg you to forgive my people and what we've done to you so many years ago!"

Magnus stood up from his seat and yelled, "Everyone except my council get out of the hall, right now! Everyone out!"

The crowd left the room in a hurry as Magnus's council circled around him. Andrew grew a little nervous as Magnus looked very stern. Magnus looked down at

Andrew and gestured for him to come closer. He reached for Andrew and laid his strong hands on his shoulders.

"King of Dunbar, this is truly a great day in our shared history! My kingdom has known of this great injustice that was put on our people, many, many years ago. We know all about what happened and how the kingdoms of Woodendale and Dunbar betrayed us. For you see, the Northlanders had two of their own soldiers in that same woods the day Bruce's men attacked the Black Hills warriors. They witnessed the entire ordeal and reported back to our king. Our great king went to your kingdom looking for justice but instead found retribution. We know all about the tale of our banishment and journey to our new home, Ice Island. We have held onto this knowledge, and our forefathers told of a day that a mighty king from Dunbar would come to our realm and beg for forgiveness. We were told on this day that two great kingdoms would reunite. We would let our past troubles be forgotten, and break bread with each other as new friends. The Kingdom of Ice Island, once known as the Northlanders, forgives you."

Andrew and Addison knelt before Magnus and thanked him. They hugged and shared a laugh. As the men were conversing, Andrew looked at the diverse council standing around King Magnus.

"My king, I do have one question for you. I notice your people are a blend of different colors. May I ask how this is so?" Andrew said.

Magnus turned toward a very tall, muscular-built man and indicated for him to speak.

"Hello, King of Dunbar. My name is Ajani. As you can see, there are many Icelanders who don't share the same white complexion as your people. We have noticeably dark skin and hair. My family is not originally from Ice Island. You see, over a hundred years ago we lived on the continent to the east. We were a peaceful, happy civilization that traded with other kingdoms regularly. Our peoples had lived on that part of the continent for over a millennium. Without any provocation or warning, our kingdom was attacked by an invader from our northeast. These horrible, nasty beings surprised us and slaughtered many of our people. Their turquoise-wearing soldiers showed no mercy, and we were no match for their cruelty. We had no choice but to flee our lands and search for a new home. Our ships got off course and we ventured farther and farther into the ocean toward the northwest. We came across this island, landed here, and the people welcomed us. They took us in and accepted us as their own. We have lived here ever since as equal partners of this kingdom."

"Yes, as you can see, Ajani's ancestors were accepted with no qualms. They are citizens and equal in every aspect on our island. We don't think of them as refugees or a separate people, we are truly one nation, one people. I believe that race, language, and outward appearance don't matter. What matters is your character, work ethic, integrity, what's in your heart! We quickly realized these people were good, honest people, and we took them in. They have been an integral part of this kingdom ever since," Magnus interjected.

"Ajani, you said turquoise-wearing soldiers from the east conquered your lands. Would these people who did this to you happen to be from the Odora Kingdom?" Andrew asked.

"Yes, but how did you know?" Ajani replied.

"Well, our island was attacked by this savage kingdom a few years ago. We also had no contact with these people before their unprovoked attack. Our whole island, all five kingdoms, united together to defeat them. We killed their king, Asiff, and they fled back to their kingdom."

"You said all five kingdoms, does that mean you've made peace with the Black Hills?" Magnus asked.

"Yes, Andrew made peace with them. He, along with the other kingdoms' kings entered their famous hall, called the pit, and formed an alliance with them. The Black Hills is now an equal partner with all the kingdoms on our island. We are truly united due to Andrew's great wisdom," Addison said.

"Why, that is great news to hear! All of God's kingdoms should be united and live in peace. I have even more respect for you knowing this, Andrew the ketea slayer!" Magnus bellowed.

"I have reason to believe that Odora is planning another attack against our island at this very minute. I needed to first come and gain forgiveness from the mighty Northlanders before I tend to this impending invasion. Now that my kingdom has gained your forgiveness, I must depart from you to defend the island," Andrew replied.

Ajani looked over at King Magnus. They shared eye contact and Ajani spoke, "Great King Magnus, after listening to these two kings of the southerly island, and having the prophecy fulfilled today by their arrival, I believe we should join with them in their time of need. I humbly ask you, mighty king, if you would allow me to take our warriors and fight alongside these peoples to protect their island from the despicable Odoran Kingdom. This would further strengthen our bond with them and bring justice for what Odora did to my people in the past. This would faithfully right a great wrong that was done to my peoples."

Magnus put his mighty hand on his chin and looked from one person to the next. He sat in thought for several minutes and then stood up towering over them.

"This day was foretold to our people by our ancestors. I believe in fate and in God. Ajani, you will get the justice your people so deserve. Andrew and Addison, you will get a new partner to share in our two islands' prosperity. YES, gather the warriors, blow the battle horns, and do away with this wicked Odora once and for all!" Magnus roared as he grabbed the hands of Addison, Andrew, and Ajani and lifted them in the air.

SEVEN

The Battle for Dunbar

I t was the night of the invasion and Sara and Finn briskly walked down the stairs to tell the war council what they had just witnessed. Sara could not believe the massive size of this invading army; it truly terrified her. She was still in shock, thinking her kingdom was under attack in the pitch darkness of night while her husband, Andrew, was away making amends for a past sin of Dunbar. Now she realized the warning Joseph had sent her and Andrew one year ago. If only Andrew was here to help, but she knew that the Dunbarians were on their own.

"Sara, what are we going to do, we can only hold them back so long?" Finn said.

"We will come up with a strategy after we appraise the council," Sara responded.

The two made it down the stairs and scurried to the great hall. Inside the hall were Timothy, Angus, Fergus, and Scott. Their faces were filled with worry as Sara approached.

"My lady, the time is becoming desperate. I fear this enemy has overwhelming numbers and will soon scale both moat walls. What did you two observe from the tower?" Angus said.

Sara looked at each man before she spoke. "It is approaching dawn, so the darkness is fading. Finn and I got a good look at the situation. This enemy, whomever it may be, has vast numbers of soldiers. We witnessed cavalry, infantry, and artillery stretching on for what seemed like eight furlongs. It is indescribable how big their numbers are. It looks as if the first wall has been conquered and they are getting desperately close to scaling the second," Sara calmly replied.

Each member of the council looked at each other and pondered the situation. The tension in the air was alarming.

"My lady, the king once told me what to do in a situation like this. When I was of age, we discussed how someday I would be king, and Father told me a secret only Kings of Dunbar know. You see, it is true that an enemy can't breach us from the flanks or from behind, due to the mountains. It is also true that they won't be able to tunnel underneath the water moat. But there is a secret passageway underneath the castle. It is a wide tunnel built by Andrew's great-great-grandfather many years ago. The purpose of this tunnel was to allow a trapped Dunbarian army to go underneath the castle, moats, and enemy, and outflank the surprising army. It is to be used only in the direst of circumstances because once used, it will no longer be a secret to our enemies. I believe the time is at hand to use this tunnel. Angus and I can lead our army through the tunnel, break out behind the enemy, and surprise attack them. This will take the pressure away from the entrance of the castle and allow us to fight them out in the open. The men are ready to fight; they are discouraged to be sitting inside the castle while the enemy is slowly breaking down the moat walls. They want to defend their homeland and fight," Fergus said.

"I have never heard of this tunnel you speak of, Fergus, but if Andrew told you so, it must be true. I am just concerned that the enemy's numbers are too great for our army, and you will not be able to defeat them," Sara sadly uttered.

"My lady, this is the only chance we have. We can't sit inside the castle and wait for them to enter it. We don't want to fight them inside with innocent women, children, and the aged. Our soldiers know the risk, and it is their duty to die for the Kingdom of Dunbar. Please, let Angus and I take the men through the tunnel and fight this horrible invader on the battlefield."

Sara looked at the other men and they all nodded their heads in agreement. They placed their hands on Angus and Fergus's shoulders, and Sara touched foreheads with Fergus.

"Your father would be so proud of you, Prince of Dunbar. Go take the men and make Dunbar proud. Scott and Timothy, I believe you should keep the guards back in the castle to protect it in case the walls are breached, and you are needed to fight here. Go, muster your men, and may God be with you all!" Sara yelled.

Angus and Fergus sprinted out of the room as Scott and Timothy discussed the best defensive strategy. Finn looked over at Sara and approached her.

"My queen. You will stay by my side. I have instructions from Andrew himself to be your protector in case of an emergency," Finn stated.

"But when did he tell you this?" the queen replied.

"Before he left, Andrew told me that if there was any sort of problems, and your life would be in danger, I was to be your personal protector. I swore an oath to him and God that I would lay down my life for you if necessary. Let's move to the observation tower so we can get a better view of what's happening outside," Finn said.

The two climbed back up the stairs with two royal guards flanking them. After the exhausting climb to the top of the stairs, the small group stood at the edge of the room and took in the carnage below. What they witnessed was stunning. For the first time in the history of Dunbar, the first moat wall had been breached. In numbers like a swarm of locusts, the enemy was scaling the second moat wall. They had brought boats to glide across the water and were using ladders to climb up the wall. Dunbarian guards were hitting these intruders with arrows, rocks, and heated tar and oils, but as quickly as one enemy soldier fell, another intruder climbed up the wall. Sara knew it was only a matter of time, their only hope was for Fergus to lead the army from the rear of the invaders and fight them on the battlefield.

At that exact moment, Angus and Fergus were leading the army through the dark tunnel underneath the carnage above. In rows of two, quiet soldiers trotted along the darkened corridor in silence. The tunnel, as Fergus mentioned, was about six feet tall by ten feet wide. It was very damp as the men trudged along the wet floor. It was pitch black inside the tunnel except for several cavalry men who were holding oil-soaked candles. Moisture seeped through the dirt walls and left puddles, which the men splattered as they trotted through. They reached the end of the tunnel, which was blocked by a huge boulder. The Dunbarians had left mighty thick sticks to move the boulder in case of situations such as this. Fergus turned around to the men and looked down the tunnel.

"Men of Dunbar, the time has come for you to do your ultimate duty to land and people. Gather your courage, your strength, and fight with me today. Fight with all your might to save our great kingdom, save your loving family, and save the queen. Fight! Fight! Fight! For Dunbar!"

At that moment the calvary men used the long sticks and moved the boulder to its side. Thousands of the best of Dunbar sprinted out of the tunnel behind the enemy's lines screaming as loud as they could. The enemy army was completely caught off guard by this tactic as the Dunbarian army swept up behind them. Fergus, Angus, and the army flew into the rear of the enemy and hacked away at the astonished army. The tide turned quickly, and Dunbar gained much-needed momentum. The enemy's army started to pull away from the castle wall to confront the danger behind them. Fergus's plan was working perfectly.

Standing at the entrance to the Dunbar castle was the leader of the enemy's army. Thoran of Odora was eagerly waiting for the last moat wall to be torn down to lead his men into the castle and gain his revenge against Dunbar. He was basking in the anticipation of being the hero of his kingdom after slaying Andrew and all the Dunbarian royalty. Startled by the commotion behind him, he was pulled from his reverie and saw a rider approaching him.

"Great King, it seems that the Dunbarian army has demonstrated their cowardice by sneaking by us and forming a resistance against our rear guard. They are killing many of our surprised soldiers. The generals in the field suggest we temporarily abandon the castle walls so we can fight their army with our superior numbers."

Thoran looked over at his Black Hills ally, Pavel, with great anger.

"What is this? You never mentioned anything about a passageway from the castle. How can this be?" Thoran shouted at Pavel.

Pavel looked at his fellow spy, Bryn (a discontent citizen from the kingdom of Lancot), with alarm. He knew he must keep his emotions and words reserved at this moment, for Thoran was unpredictable when handling bad news.

"My king, we have never heard of this before. It must have been a secret held by Dunbar for many generations. Nobody in either one of our kingdoms has ever heard of any secret passageway. The Dunbarians are clever, sneaky people. It is no surprise they would find a cowardly way to evade our army."

"I am greatly disappointed in you and your ignorance of our enemy. But I will deal with this later. For now, we will turn away from the castle to confront our greater threat. After we slaughter this army, we will return to the castle and destroy it. Then we will go level by level and kill all the pathetic swine of Dunbar!"

Thoran rode off with the two island traitors and met quickly with his generals. They decided to put the full brunt of their army against the Dunbarian army. The two armies clashed, and Dunbar pushed into the heart of the Odoran army. After about half an hour of fighting, the Dunbar army's momentum was halted. Slowly and methodically Odora's soldiers gained ground. Their enormous advantage of numbers played out on the battlefield, and they started to engulf the Dunbarian army. Fergus and Angus had led their army courageously, but they knew they would succumb to the sheer size of the Odoran army.

EIGHT

The Protector of Dunbar

Sara and Finn were watching in horror from the castle observation tower as all of this took place. They were astonished at the bravery of the Dunbarian army and Fergus's leadership but could see that their lack of numbers could not stand up to the size of the enemy army. Sara knew she had to do something, or the entire Dunbar army would perish. She looked at Finn who appeared utterly frightened.

"Finn, go and find Timothy. The two of you need to block off the tunnel entrance to the castle so the enemy can't use it. Go, go now!" Sara yelled.

As Finn flew down the stairs, Sara got onto her knees and prayed to God.

"Lord God, please give me the strength for what I am about to do. If it is your will, let me save Dunbar. All is possible with you. I believe in you, love you, and ask for your guidance. Amen."

The battle for Dunbar was winding down, and Dunbar was losing quickly. Fergus and his men were surrounded on all sides by the larger Odoran army. Thoran and his co-conspirators were watching the demise of Dunbar with glee.

"It will only be a matter of time before my mighty army demolishes this cowardly, weak enemy. Then we will circle back and break down the last castle wall and end the line of Dunbar forever!" Thoran shouted.

As Thoran finished speaking, a loud horn blast resonated through the air.

"What sound is that?" Thoran asked.

Pavel looked at Bryn and then at Thoran.

"That blast is coming from the Horn of Kings. Each of the five kings on the island possesses one of these horns. When used, it means a king wants the battle to stop to hold a one-on-one fight between two kings. It seems that Andrew is calling you out to meet you on the battlefield. I think it's a mistake; we almost have their army defeated," Pavel explained.

"What? And miss my opportunity to wipe away my enemy. I will meet this gutless Andrew in front of my entire army and avenge my father's death. Tell the generals to have the men stop fighting. This will be the end of Dunbar! Ha, ha!" Thoran screamed.

Thoran's generals gathered around him, helping him armor up. He had two long, golden swords with turquoise-colored handles attached to his back. Several small knives were hidden in his pants, and a turtle-shaped shield encircled his arm. He mounted his white Arabian horse and sped off toward the castle with Pavel and Bryn flanking him.

The great door of the Dunbar castle dropped down harshly on the ground. As the morning sun rose above the horizon, a stunning sight stepped forward. The Queen of Dunbar stood, glowing in the early morning sun. She stood erect, blasting the Horn of Kings with one arm and in the other had a short shield. Sara was wearing a golden-colored suit of armor from head to toe with two long, silver swords crisscrossed on her back. Her beautiful sun-colored hair was twisted into braids that stretched to her lower back. She had a serious, earnest look on her face. Sara slowly walked away from the castle and toward the battlefield. Dunbarians looking from inside the castle were stunned, and many had tears falling down their faces as they witnessed this unbelievable sight.

Thoran approached on his horse. He got within ten feet of her and dismounted. Pavel and Bryn were right behind him. Thoran was perplexed to see Sara holding the horn, for he was expecting to see Andrew.

"What is this? Where is Andrew and who are you?" Thoran asked.

"I am Sara, Queen of Dunbar. I have come to meet our invader in person. Who are you, and why are you attacking our innocent kingdom?" Sara responded.

"INNOCENT! I think not! Your traitorous kingdom killed my father, Asiff. I am here to seek revenge for my kingdom Odora and kill King Andrew. Where is that weak leader of Dunbar? Why did he send his wife out to defend his kingdom instead of being brave enough to fight? Is he a coward?" Thoran asked impatiently.

"So, now I know who you are. Asiff wasn't an honorable man. He attacked our island for illegitimate reasons. He was power-hungry and angry. You don't need to go down his path. You can—"

"STOP, witch! I don't need to listen to your ramblings. My father was a great king, and he was going to rid this island of weak, deplorable people. It would've become a great, strong part of the Odoran Kingdom. Now, where is Andrew? Why won't he come out and fight me?" Thoran asked.

"Andrew is not here. He is not on the island at this moment. It was I who blasted the horn," Sara responded.

"I don't believe you, witch. Andrew can't be that cowardly," Thoran replied.

"I am not lying. Andrew is not on the island. I am here as the leader of Dunbar. Now, take your men, leave the island, and never come back. I will spare your life. Repent and live a productive life. Go now and let us be. We are peaceful people who follow the Lord's will," Sara said.

"She's not lying. She would not blast the horn if Andrew was here. He must not be on the island. No king on this island would betray the sacred tradition of the Horn of Kings," Pavel said.

Thoran laughed out loud and pulled Bryn and Pavel toward him. He looked toward Sara.

"We are not going anywhere until we destroy your castle and lands. We will burn your churches down and kill your people. First, my two friends and I are going to kill you and gut you like a pig. Then we will finish off your pitiful army, and finally destroy your castle," Thoran shrieked.

Bryn and Pavel both looked at each other with puzzled looks. Neither man could believe what they just heard.

"King, we agreed to plot this invasion together. We will conquer Dunbar together, fight their soldiers, but I can't attack a woman. We can capture her instead, but I will not be a part of fighting her," Bryn said.

Thoran looked at Bryn with disgust. He then looked over at Pavel.

"Are you also unworthy of me? I have given you everything you wanted; the island will be ours after this morning. You just need courage to follow my plan. She blew the horn; she knew the consequences. I will kill her and then her kingdom, and when Andrew arrives, we will destroy him as well!" Thoran screamed.

Pavel didn't say anything in reply. Bryn approached Thoran to talk sense into him and as soon as he got within Thoran's reach, Thoran quickly thrust a knife into Bryn's stomach. Bryn fell over on the ground as Sara gasped.

"Well, Prince of Black Hills, what about you? Are you with me or against me?" Thoran asked.

"I can't be a part of this, Thoran. I didn't come here to fight women; it is unworthy of my people and heritage. It is not honorable. Especially fighting her two-on-one. That's not heroic! I will fight the Dunbarian soldiers but not the queen," Pavel replied.

"Fine, I will deal with you later. Now I'm going to finish off the queen," Thoran laughed as he spoke.

The Odoran King and Dunbarian Queen faced each other. Both reached behind their necks and pulled out their swords. Thoran charged at Sara and swung wildly. His sword breezed by her head and then she kicked him in the stomach. A sword thrust by Sara was thwarted by his shield. He quickly circled around and went on the attack again. Every movement by Thoran was easily brushed aside by the agile queen. Her reflexes were quicker than his and she had great control of her weapons. For the next twenty minutes, Thoran attacked, and Sara easily defended.

"Who trained you, witch? I can tell you have been formally trained in weapons," Thoran asked.

"I am not a witch! Stop calling me that, for I'm a woman of God. Andrew has taught me everything he knows about combat. He has spent many years training me to fight, and I am skillful in a variety of weapons. Nobody knows about my training except Andrew, but as you can see, you are no match for me. Surrender or I will need to unnecessarily harm you. You don't need to follow through with this. I will spare your men; you can leave in peace and never come back to this island," Sara responded.

"NEVER!" Thoran screamed as his body was uncontrollably shaking.

He ran at her again, swords flailing in the air. Sara effortlessly blocked both thrusts and got a direct hit on Thoran. He fell to the ground, dropping one of his swords. Now he was down to one weapon. He got up, visibly frustrated. This time he slowly approached, raising his sword above his head. As he stabbed forward, Sara dodged his blow and grabbed his arm. She quickly twisted it harshly, and Thoran yelled out in pain. He dropped his sword and tripped on a rock, landing on his face.

"King of Odora. You are beaten! Surrender now or pay the consequences," Sara spoke with authority.

At that moment, a great rustling noise was heard from the hills to the east. As Sara, Thoran, and Pavel looked in that direction, an army was riding up on the summit of the hill. There were thousands of men in armor sitting on sturdy horses. Leading this army was Andrew, and next to him was a dark-skinned man wearing a tunic with a cross on it. In fact, almost all these soldiers wore these same tunics. This army spread out and engulfed the entire summit of the hill. They stared down menacingly at the Odoran army.

"It's Andrew! He has done it! He brought back the Northlanders with him. We are saved! Thank God, we are saved! Oh, Andrew, I knew you would prevail," Sara gleefully shouted.

Thoran used Sara's distracted state and grabbed sand from the ground. He thrust a handful of it into her face and rolled over to grab one of his swords lying on the ground. Sara was blinded by this cowardly act and held one sword out in front of her. She could not see anything in front of her and was in grave danger. Thoran approached her with a sword held over his head. Right at the moment he was going to swing down and end her life, a loud thud was heard. Thoran groaned and looked down at his chest. Pavel had thrown a short sword through the air, making contact with Thoran. The Odoran King fell to both knees, crying out in shock. He fell face-first to the ground, and the king was dead. Sara was screaming, unaware of what had happened. She was still blinded by the sand, and when Pavel touched her shoulders, she cried out in terror.

"No, Queen Sara. It is I, Pavel from the Black Hills. I will not hurt you. I just ended Thoran's life, as he was about to kill you. You are okay, you won the fight, and the threat is over. Please, Queen, I was wrong. I never imagined that he could be so evil and attack a woman. He was not an honorable man. I should have never trusted him; I am so sorry. Can you forgive me?" Pavel stated.

Sara was a little confused and apprehensive about what had just happened. She slowly backed away from Pavel's voice. Her eyes were watering, and she still couldn't see very well.

"Just let me get my bearings," Sara said. "Who are you again?"

"I am Pavel, son of Marko. Our ancestors date back to the original Black Hills Kingdom. I was seduced by Thoran's talk of revenge and power. I was jealous of Sergio's relationship with Andrew. I am ashamed that I took part in his evil plans. I apologize for ever getting caught up with Thoran and the Odoran Kingdom. Again, my queen, can you please forgive my actions?" Pavel stated.

"Take me to Andrew, young Black Hills warrior, and we can discuss later your dealings," Sara responded.

The two of them rode off toward the battlefield and spotted Andrew in the distance. As they got closer, Sara's heart and soul ached to see her husband. When they were less than ten feet from each other, they both dismounted and ran toward each other. Andrew lifted Sara in the air and hugged her.

"Oh, how I missed you, Andrew! I prayed for this day when we would be reunited with each other. Don't let me go!" Sara said.

"I will never let you go, my queen!" Andrew yelled before kissing her.

"Are these the Northlanders you went looking for?" Sara asked.

"Yes, these are our new friends and allies, the Northlander Kingdom. I met their King Magnus, and he has forgiven our kingdom for what we did to them centuries ago. We are welcoming them back to our island, and they have come to our aid in this battle against Odora," Andrew responded.

Ajani bowed to the queen and kissed her hand.

"It is an honor to meet you, your husband could not stop talking about you," Ajani said.

The combined army of Northlanders and Dunbarians were in the process of routing the enemy. The two kingdoms' armies fought together like they were one people, a truly amazing feat playing out in front of the armies. What was left of the Odoran army had laid down their arms and surrendered. As Andrew, Sara, Pavel, and Ajani were watching this transpire, Fergus and Angus rode to the group.

"Father, Father, it so great to see you again!" Fergus said as he jumped off the horse and father and son hugged.

"Father, these horrible, arrogant, people attacked us without provocation. They had us nearly defeated before you and these friends of yours arrived. NOW is the time to end their threat forever. We must slaughter the remainder of their army so they can never harm our people again!" Fergus angrily stated.

"No, Fergus, that is not the way. We don't kill soldiers who have surrendered and laid down their weapons. We must put them in the dungeons. You know the scripture, Proverbs 25:21-22. 'If your enemy is hungry, give him food to eat; if he is thirsty, give him water to drink. In doing this, you will heap burning coals on his head, and the Lord will reward you,'" Sara responded.

"How can you be so forgiving to these evil people? They almost destroyed our kingdom and castle with all its people. They don't deserve mercy," Fergus yelled.

"Did we deserve the mercy that God gave us when he washed away our sins through Jesus's death and resurrection?" Sara responded.

"No, my son, the queen is correct. We can't kill these men; we would be no better than them. We will take them to the dungeons and hold them there. We will get down to the bottom of how this terrible attack occurred and learn from it," Andrew stated.

"Fools! You are wrong. I will not take part in this." Fergus mounted his horse and rode away from the royalty.

"Let him be, he will cool down. His anger is understandable considering what the Odorans have done to our island these past years," Andrew said.

The next night was a glorious night in the great hall of the Dunbar castle. Every long table was full of men and women sharing stories, food and drink, and laughter. A great feast of hog, lamb, and seafood was on every platter. Bread and mead were being devoured by Northlanders and Dunbarians alike. Andrew and Sara were seated next to Addison and Ajani. Sara looked at her husband with fondness and smiled. Andrew stood up and got the attention of all in the hall.

"With great sadness, I would like us all to acknowledge the dead who bravely defended home and people. A great number of our soldiers perished defeating this horrible enemy. Please, let's raise a glass to our fallen comrades and then have a moment of silence to honor them," Andrew bellowed.

Northlanders and Dunbarians alike grimly looked at each other and acknowledged the dead. After a long minute of remembrance, Andrew spoke again.

"I would also like to speak of a great new occurrence. Many years ago, our kingdom was at fault for banishing a peaceful kingdom off our island," Andrew said.

The people of Dunbar all looked at each other with puzzled faces. A sixth kingdom? How was that possible?

Andrew continued, "I was gone from Dunbar to right this wrong and bring our two kingdoms back together. With great happiness, I can tell you that the bond between our kingdoms has been reunited. Their great king, Magnus, has forgiven us. We will share in the riches of our kingdoms and be true allies with each other. They came to our aid at a time of desperation and fought with us to defeat the Odorans. Without their help, this victory would not have been possible. Please, all Dunbarians, raise your glasses and give a demonstration of our gratitude for the Kingdom of Northland!" Andrew shouted.

The great hall erupted in celebration and jubilation. People hugged and laughed, and Ajani beamed with delight as he witnessed his people being appreciated.

Andrew stood and quieted the crowd one more time. Looking over at his wife, Sara, he asked her to stand. The look of love on his face was undeniable to all in the hall.

"Finally, I would like to say a word about the Queen of Dunbar. Years ago, after the loss of my wife and mother by that traitor Malcolm, I was in a dark place. Through the grace of God, I was able to meet a young, beautiful woman. Sara became my wife and your queen. She brought joy, peace, and happiness not only to my life but to the lives of all Dunbarians. She is unselfish, joyful, and brave. She has sacrificed for this kingdom numerous times. After returning and defeating the Odorans, it has been told of her great courage and dedication to the people of this kingdom. When our people were at their most dire time, Sara donned her armor and blew the Horn of Kings. She met the enemy's king in the field of battle and defeated him. Without this intervention by her, our army was about to be conquered. She knew that they needed more time. She bravely stepped out of the castle and gave us that precious time as she fought Thoran. I cannot say enough about our lovely, fearless, God-fearing queen. All of us, stand and acknowledge Sara, the Protector of Dunbar!!!" Andrew shouted.

The whole room stood up and shouted enthusiastically, "Protector, Protector, Protector!" Men and women walked up to her and kissed her ring. Ajani, Addison, and all the royalty surrounded her so they could individually thank her. It was a great night to be in the large hall of the Dunbar castle.

The next afternoon, Sara and Andrew were out in the Dunbarian graveyard. During their jubilant night of celebration, Andrew's uncle Collin had peacefully passed. Andrew was told later that morning, and the king and queen decided to look in the graveyard for a spot to bury his uncle. Sara was admiring some primrose and thistle plants while Andrew was deep in thought. As the couple was eyeing a potential location next to a young birch tree, the head royal guard, Scott, was racing toward them on his sturdy horse. Scott's face was deep red, and sweat was pouring down his face. He jumped off his horse and ran toward the king and queen as fast as he could.

"King Andrew, King Andrew! I am so sorry to disturb you, but this could not wait. It is about the dungeons!" Scott said as he struggled to catch his breath.

"What about the dungeons?" Andrew asked.

Scott looked very nervous. "All the prisoners have been killed. The doors to the dungeon were wide open this morning. When Timothy and I entered, the prisoners' bodies were all lined up near the wall. They had been killed sometime in the night and all the sentry guards were missing."

Andrew and Sara looked at each other with great concern and then back at Scott.

Scott looked at the king and then said, "There is one more thing, King Andrew. Your son, Fergus. He is missing, and nobody knows where he is!"

Nine

Disorder

What!!! Fergus, my oldest son, the Prince of Dunbar is missing! How? When was he seen last?" Andrew asked.

"I noticed he wasn't at the victory celebration in the great hall, but I thought he was still angry from our conversation and just needed some time to cool off," Sara responded.

"Yes, he has always been a feisty one, I've told him many times that his temper would get the best of him. I hope he hasn't done something rash," Andrew said.

"We don't know his whereabouts. Nobody has seen him since the battle concluded. I think we should go down to the dungeons and investigate further. Maybe we can find some clues as to his whereabouts," Scott replied.

"Yes, I agree. There could be something that was missed when investigating," Andrew said.

The three of them hastily moved on to the castle and had a squad of guards accompany them to the dungeons. These guards were experienced in performing search parties and used dogs to sniff out missing or escaped people. The dogs were a hound breed, notorious on the island for their great sense of smell and easy-going nature.

The dungeons of Dunbar are on the bottom level of the castle in the southeast section. When the castle was built centuries ago, great detail was given to having dungeons where external or internal threats could be held. To reach them, you must descend from the ground level of the castle on cold, damp stairs dimly lit by a few lamps that give the climb down a dark and eerie feeling. These stairs wind around in circles and the air temperature drops the lower you descend. By the time you reach the bottom of the stairs, you have descended over thirty feet below ground.

Sara had never gone down to the dungeons before so when she entered the "jail" area, she was astonished at how many cells there were. Over twenty-five cells were located here with iron gates hanging open as the royal group walked into the large area. Sara and Andrew could see the dead Odoran prisoners all lined up in a row next to the southeastern wall of the dungeons. The prisoners had spears thrust into their torsos, and you could still see their shocked expressions as they lay on the cold, damp ground in bunches. It truly was a massacre.

"What happened here? Where are the guards who were on duty, and how could they have let this happen?" Andrew asked.

"There are always eight men on duty, six at this level and two near the entrance at the top level. None of the eight men on duty have been found," Scott replied.

At that moment, a rustling noise came from the group of dead prisoners, and the guards immediately formed a phalanx to shield the king and queen. As the guards moved slowly toward a pile of about five deceased prisoners, they saw a leg slowly moving from underneath and heard a faint voice. As Scott gingerly moved the clump of dead bodies, a guard who had been pinned down by the weight of the men was struggling to move his body. The guards quickly grabbed him and lifted him into the air. He had obviously been wounded and was very weak.

"Who are you, what is your name, guardsman?" Scott screamed at him.

"Water, can you please give me some water?" he said with a weak, gravelly voice. The guards held a canteen above him and let water trickle into his dry mouth. After about a minute, the short, blonde-haired guard raised his head and looked around the room. His eyes met Andrew's, and he got down on one knee to bow to the king and queen.

"I am Robert, guardsman low class of the dungeon, Your Highness. I am ashamed of what happened here while I was on watch. May it be allowed for me to speak freely of what happened here last night, oh mighty king?" Robert weakly stated.

As he tried standing up, he wobbled, and two guards had to hold him steady. Blood was trickling out of his lower leg and his breathing was labored.

"Get him some more water and some of our dried apricots for sustenance. It looks like he could fall over from exhaustion at any second," Andrew demanded.

They gave the poor guard some food and water, bandaged his leg, and in five minutes time he was strong enough to speak.

"My name is Robert, son of Aiden, and our family's heritage goes back centuries in the Kingdom of Dunbar. I come from a long line of guardsmen in duty to the king. I have been assigned the role of dungeon guardsman for five years under royal guard Ronan's command," Robert said.

"Yes, Ronan is the head guard in the dungeons," Scott said.

"Last night, early in the night, we were on duty. All of us were discussing how great a celebration it must be in the great hall and how we all were envious of the guards with that detail. The prisoners were well-behaved and quiet, mostly ashamed of their defeat on the battlefield. We could hear voices and the loud pounding of feet descending the stairs. Prince Fergus walked out of the staircase with several men I had never seen before, along with the two guards on higher-level duty. Fergus and Ronan spoke cordially for several minutes and then the unthinkable happened. Fergus stabbed Ronan in the chest with a dagger and the men accompanying him attacked several of the unsuspecting guards. My fellow guards were quickly overpowered, and what is worse, the two guards stationed at the higher level were part of the plot," Robert calmly stated.

"How did you avoid being attacked?" Scott asked

"One of Fergus's men hit me over the head, and I blacked out. When I finally awoke, I was lying under the dead soldiers. I was weak and groggy, for I must have been lying there all night," Robert said.

"You didn't see the soldiers being executed then?" Scott said.

"No, I did not," Robert replied.

"And you're sure it was Fergus who was in the dungeons?" Andrew asked.

Robert looked like he didn't want to answer, he slowly looked away from the king but finally answered.

"Yes, I'm sure it was Fergus. I am deeply sorry, my king," Robert replied.

Sara gasped as she heard Robert's accusation.

"If this is true, it is deeply disturbing. My son not only disobeyed my orders but more importantly has done the unthinkable, betraying his kingdom and God's laws," Andrew stated.

"These men that you speak of who were with Fergus, what did they look like?" Sara asked.

"Well, they had black cloaks on with dark, black hair. One of them was very tall and he had a devious expression. My body felt cold when I looked into his piercing, dark, eyes, and I had to look away. He was standing by Fergus the whole time and whispering things into his ear," Robert replied.

"Grigori! That deceitful man has been spending too much time with Fergus these last several months. I never have trusted him," Sara responded.

"Grigori, really? I didn't know he and Fergus were such close companions," Andrew stated.

"Yes, the two have spent a lot of time together while you were gone, and I warned Fergus about his nature. Something is wrong about him; I just know it," Sara said.

"Scott, if Fergus and Grigori did this, how were they able to climb back up to the main level and not be seen?" Andrew asked.

"Well, if Robert is correct and the two guards stationed at the entrance to the dungeon were part of the plot, they would have unguarded access to the main level of the castle. Our only question now is, where is Fergus? Has he been seen by anyone in the castle?" Sara said.

"I will have all the guards who were posted at the castle walls interviewed immediately, and we will have the dogs start a scent hunt. We also need to bury the dead and honor our lost guards, especially Ronan," Scott replied.

The dogs were brought over to the area where the dead soldiers lay and then brought to Fergus's room on the second level of the castle. His room was very bare, with only a few trinkets and items of clothing tossed about. The dogs were led to the clothes and took a long, slow sniff. They then immediately started barking and were excitedly leading their handlers out of the room.

Sara looked at Andrew with sorrow in her eyes. She reached for his hand and held it tight.

"My love, I can't believe Fergus would do such a thing. Killing innocent prisoners, attacking our own guards. What has come over him?" Andrew sadly stated.

"Andrew, Grigori's power of persuasion is not to be understated. He may have Fergus under some spell. I knew when I last spoke to him of Grigori's influence over him that there could be serious problems in the future. Andrew, they have spent a lot of time together, who knows what Grigori has filled Fergus's mind with," Sara said.

"I must find Fergus so I can get to the bottom of what's happened. Please stay here, Protector," Andrew said.

Sara hugged her husband. She knew this wasn't going to be as easy as Andrew thought, but she found it amusing when he used her new nickname.

"Good luck, my love, we will do whatever is needed to protect Dunbar and bring Fergus back into the good graces of God," Sara said.

TEN

Sinister Meeting

It was a dark, cold night in the kingdom of the Black Hills. Twenty years before Fergus's betrayal, a sinister meeting took place. Deep inside the Black Hills Kingdom, in an area so remote and wild that the king's entourage barely ever crossed into it, was a hamlet of several families. A few families lived in huts or inside caves in this barren, windy, dry landscape. The people here were so wild in nature that they would attack anyone who ventured into their land. Infants born here were inspected, and if found with any defects, they would be tossed from the highest hill into a pit, abandoned, and left to die. Buzzards, crows, and ravens could be seen aloft in dry, leafless trees. It was common for people here to scavenge and steal from other Black Hills villages. There was no real farming because the land was depleted of any minerals and resources. Some of the men ventured into the caves of the hills to mine for metals like iron and tin. Even the king at that time, Vlad the Destroyer, had never bothered to enter this wild area, for these people never gave any of their young men to serve in the king's army. There were even whispers of cannibalism in this area but no true evidence, only rumors. It was better to leave these miserable, angry people alone and let them live out their lives.

On this night, a night in late January when the snow and cold keep all creatures in by a fire, an ominous meeting was taking place. Inside one of the caves in this hamlet lived an old, decrepit man named Nikolai. Nobody knew his actual age, but all agreed he must be over a hundred years old. Now this would be quite a feat, for most people living in the Black Hills only reached their thirties or forties before they died. Nikolai had wispy white hair that was as thin as his long, white beard. When his mouth opened, only two crooked, yellow-stained teeth could be seen. His skin was wrinkled and leathery looking, and his long, yellow fingernails had black muck embedded inside them. His cave was sparse, except for several old-looking books and black cauldrons that were sitting over glowing fires. Nikolai was looking up at a much younger Black Hills man and giving him directions. This younger man kept rubbing his hands to keep them warm and stretching his legs to keep the blood flowing on such a cold night.

"Now, my young follower, I have taught you everything I know over these last few years. You are truly ready to take my place and become the most powerful man on this island. Remember, before making your move in the future, first, you must grow an army of followers only loyal to you, not the king. You must make the king trust you and believe you are his loyal subject. Once you have laid the groundwork, then you can show who you really are. My time here has almost ended, we must do the ceremony before I pass. Come here, boy, and give me your hand," Nikolai said.

The follower approached slowly, almost apprehensively. When he got close, Nikolai grabbed his arm with such strength and vitality, the man was shocked. Nikolai placed both of their arms into the cauldron and held them there as he chanted some words. After a short time, he lifted both of their arms into the air and placed a vial in the man's hand before also taking one into his own. Both men drank from the vials. Stomach pain occurred instantly, and they rolled on the ground in agony. After at least five minutes, the two men slowly regained their senses and stood. Nikolai again grabbed the man's arms and raised them in the air.

"It is time, time for my protégé to become the master! Take the knowledge and skills I have taught you and exert your power over this island. Remember, boy, what is the most important lesson I taught you?" Nikolai shouted.

"That power is most important. That chaos and disunity must always be promoted, and love is untrue. God is to be smitten from this island and the kingdoms should never be at peace. That I will control the minds of the kings and peoples of this island," the man retorted.

"YES, YES! YOU HAVE LEARNED WELL. TAKE MY TEACHINGS, MY KNOWLEDGE, AND WREAK HAVOC ON THIS ISLAND. MAKE EVERYONE SUFFER AND BRING PAIN TO ALL THE KINGDOMS, ESPECIALLY ARROGANT DUNBAR. GO NOW, GRIGORI, GO, AND FULFILL YOUR DESTINY. GRIGORI, YOUR NAME WILL BE FEARED FOR GENERATIONS!" Nikolai laughed hysterically.

The next day, the old man expired, and his body was thrown into the pit along with all the dead in the area. The people in this land were so cruel, lazy, and devoid of any feelings or love, that they wouldn't bother burying their dead. They let the buzzards and vermin take care of their bodies.

"Prince Fergus, listen to me, don't have second thoughts. What you have done needed to be done. Your father has dishonored his kingdom by showing weakness and allowing these new people back onto the land that is rightfully Dunbar's. He shows more interest in Sergio (King of Black Hills) and these new people than you and your fellow Dunbarians. He spends all his time building churches and roads in the Black Hills when he should be in his own kingdom. He must be replaced by the true leader of Dunbar, you! Only you can restore the glory of Dunbar, only your strong leadership and determination can bring back this kingdom," Gregori said in a demanding voice.

Fergus listened to his advisor and nodded his head. When he looked into Grigori's eyes, his mind became clouded. It was as if he was in a fog and couldn't think straight, but he believed his mind was clear.

"Yes, you are correct. My father has failed our people. When we needed him most, he was away for months giving away lands to some far-off kingdom. He no longer has the ability to truly lead; he has become soft. The queen has too much influence on him, she has weakened him," Fergus replied.

"YES! The queen is his weakness, but he has allowed her to be so. You, Prince Fergus, will not allow distractions. You will become a true king and will replace your father and rule with an iron fist. Your name will go down in history as one of the great kings on this island," Grigori stated.

"What should I do now, my loyal advisor?" Fergus asked.

"You should continue to rally allies to your cause and after we have enough men for a strong army, send a message to your father asking him to meet. At this meeting we will give him an ultimatum; either relinquish the throne to you or face your army in battle. I believe Andrew will not risk killing his own kin. After taking the throne from your father, you must take the fight to that false King Sergio and the Black Hills Kingdom," Grigori hissed.

"Once again, your advice is so accurate. Let me meet with my lieutenants in the field and we will move on our plans," Fergus said as he walked out of the room.

Grigori smiled and laughed out loud. He thought to himself how easily his plans were playing out, and he summoned his subordinates. These wicked men were indistinguishable from each other. All wore black cloaks with hoods over their heads, which concealed their pale, ugly faces. They had long, greasy hair and dark eyes. The most disturbing aspect was the long, yellow fingernails that reached outward from their fingers. They rarely spoke unless spoken to, but their lust for evil and power was equal to their master Grigori. Grigori had trained each of these foul creatures from birth and they were completely loyal to him.

"My friends, the time is at hand. Our plans have worked perfectly. Fergus has played right into my hands. He is so confused and irrational right now he doesn't understand his actions. Soon there will be war, civil war, and it will tear this island apart. Once all the kingdoms are fighting with each other, there will be a vacuum of power that I can use to my advantage. Men will fall and populations will dwindle. The people will be looking for someone to put an end to the chaos, and that's when we will step in and control the minds of all the kings who are left on the island. After we have full control of the royalty, we will be the true rulers of the island. We will tear down their institutions, culture, and especially their churches. We will reshape people's minds so they will not realize that their fear has led to their demise. Oh, it is so close to happening! I can feel it in my bones!" Grigori screamed.

A week later a letter arrived for Andrew. The royal carrier of letters, William (the former zookeeper and cousin to Andrew) came running up the stairs to the king's room.

"My lord, I have a letter for you. It is addressed from Fergus!" William shouted.

Andrew took the letter abruptly out of William's hand and ripped it open. He stood stoically erect and read the letter without saying a word. After finishing the letter Andrew huffed in annoyance and slammed his hand down onto the nearby table.

"I can't believe what has happened to my son! He is claiming that I have broken the trust of the people of Dunbar and am responsible for the attack from the Odorans. He is demanding that I meet him on the Plains of Daniel in one month's time so I can relinquish my throne to him. BLASPHEMY! I brought peace and unity to the island. I left the island to restore honor and dignity to Dunbar after the sins of our past; the sin of banishing the Northlanders, and now we are friends again. The Black Hills have become as strong an ally as the Woodlanders. The island is whole, and he is destroying the unity that we have. This Grigori must be controlling his mind. When we meet in one month, I will convince Fergus of his madness and this unholy quest for war. Father and son will be united again," Andrew bellowed.

"He has unfortunately gathered malcontents from all kingdoms, my lord. If you can't convince him to stop, this war could destroy the island. All kingdoms on the island will be in disarray," William replied.

"Yes, William, I must meet with Fergus and talk sense into him. I must convince him that he is being led down the wrong path by this Grigori. Send couriers to all the kings so they can be present at this meeting. Go now, my kin!" Andrew said.

During that month, both Andrew and Fergus worked hard to bolster their numbers. Fergus used Grigori's cunning language to convince other disgruntled islanders that Andrew needed to be replaced as king due to his softening, aloof attitude. Slowly he was gaining men to his cause and at each meeting, Fergus was becoming more confident in his ability to displace his father as king. Likewise, Andrew was meeting with all his ally kings to shore up their support and displace any rumors that Grigori was spreading throughout the island. He was confident that the overall number of men supporting his cause would discourage Fergus and bring him back to reality. Neither man was ready to face the consequences of this civil unrest.

ELEVEN

Devil's Lair

The day of the meeting had arrived, and both sides rode out to the Plains of Daniel and squared off against each other. The plains were located east of Woodendale and west of Lancot, a place where many battles had been fought in the past. The plains rose to an elevation of over 1500 feet above sea level, giving it a vantage point high enough for the army to see for miles. Andrew took the Woodendale king, Elaran, with him and started toward Fergus. Fergus nodded to Grigori, and they rode out to meet Andrew and Elaran.

"Father, I am glad you read my letter and have decided to follow through with this meeting. It has become obvious to me over the last years that you have grown soft in your old age and no longer have the best interest of Dunbar at heart. You may believe so, but you don't. I reluctantly agreed with you to allow our old enemies, the Black Hills, to become an ally, but when you abandoned our kingdom for months to betray our shared kingdom's land to these outsiders, the Northlanders, that was the last affront for me. We have no business giving up our shared lands, Woodendale and Dunbar, to these peoples. To make matters worse, because of your quest to see these people, our kingdom was almost destroyed by the Odorans. After we did defeat them, you were too shortsighted to do what was needed, to eliminate the remaining Odoran soldiers. It is time, Father, for you to do what is best for the kingdom of Dunbar, which is to step down as king. Abdicate the throne and allow me to rule, I have not lost the way. I will be the strong king that Dunbar and the entire island need," Fergus stated boldly.

"YESSS, my exalted one. Well-spoken, spoken like a true king," Gregori added.

"Hold your forked tongue, you snake! You have warped my son's mind against me, he would never be doing this if it wasn't for your devious mind tricks," Andrew yelled.

"No, Father, Grigori has shown me the error of my ways and given me the ability to see for the first time that you have failed as king. This must be done so Dunbar can be restored to its greatness," Fergus responded.

"Young prince, you don't really believe this. Your father is a great king and only has the best interests of all the kingdoms at heart. He has brought true unity to this island. We now have all six kingdoms in harmony. You must see that?" Elaran stated.

"Look around you, great King of the Woodendale Kingdom. Do you see how many men have rallied to my cause? You must notice that I have men from every kingdom who believe as I do. There are even men and women from your kingdom who have joined with us," Fergus replied.

Grigori grabbed Fergus's arm and whispered something into his ear. Fergus nodded in agreement and looked at his father.

"If you will not agree to abdicate, then the crown must be taken by force. We will have our army here at this spot in one month. Give up the throne or it will be taken by force!" Fergus confidently stated.

"YOU HAVE GONE MAD MY SON! I will never abdicate for I have done nothing wrong. I have brought unity and peace to the island; all the kingdoms are allies with each other. There is no more need for war! You are lost, Fergus, please listen to logic. I will be here in one month with a mighty, united army from all the kingdoms. We will show you how "soft" I've become," Andrew shouted.

As the four were ready to ride away, Grigori turned back and looked Andrew in the eyes. He smiled a wicked, evil smile that alarmed the great king. Andrew could feel the evil resonate within his bones as he looked back at Grigori.

"You did what?! No, Andrew, that can't be the answer. You can't go to war against your own son. It will destroy Dunbar and the entire island. Why couldn't you have reasoned with him? You must call off this upcoming battle, bring him to the castle and we can talk reason with him," Sara pleaded.

"NO! I gave him a chance. He won't listen to reason, Gregori has poisoned his mind. I've been more than patient. I can't allow an affront on my power to go unchecked. If I back down I will be seen as weak, and more people will join his cause. I must follow through and defeat his army on the battlefield," Andrew replied.

"This is madness, darling. Can't you see that you are both headed for a disaster? Are you willing to kill your own son? Stop this, call off the forthcoming battle," Sara stated.

"No, it is too late. My mind is made up, leave me to my thoughts," Andrew gloomily stated.

Sara walked off in disgust. Why couldn't these intelligent men see that they were going to destroy not just Dunbar, but the entire island? All the great work that had been done to unify the island would be destroyed, and chaos would come to the people. She had to do something to stop this, but what could she do? She paced the room thinking of ideas when her cross necklace thumped her chest.

"That's it! I will pray for guidance and go see the angel, Joseph. I'm sure he will provide an answer," Sara whispered to herself.

A week later Sara was on a journey to the green emerald located in the Blue Forest. Finn had heard Sara speak about her upcoming travel, and he insisted on going with her as protection. Finn had reminded her that he was chosen by Andrew to be her protector and her protector he would be. Sara reluctantly agreed but insisted that he must leave her as she went into the forest, for only Andrew and she could enter that part of the forest and know the whereabouts of the emerald (and the angel). The two ventured off during a fine early autumn sunrise and made it to the forest by midday.

"Now, Finn, you promised to stay here and wait for me," Sara said to the king's cousin.

"Yes, but I don't understand why I can't go into the forest with you. There are dangerous animals in there, remember those dreadful coal cats that attacked your division this past year?" Finn responded.

"I'll never forget that horrible day, Finn. But you just can't go with me, under the orders of the King and Queen of Dunbar. Stay here and I'll be back in several hours, I promise," Sara ordered.

Finn hunkered down and set up a camp while Sara slowly entered the Blue Forest. For hours, Sara walked through the forest using her memory of the location that Andrew and she found. Sara had an outstanding memory and in no time was on the trail. As she came to the undergrowth of trees that encircled the stream and emerald, Sara swallowed and took a deep breath.

She was nervous since she had never been here before without Andrew. But she knew this was the right thing to do and she walked forward. She crawled under the trees and swiftly walked to the stream. She pulled out the green emerald and instantly a bright light showed above her. Sara had to shield her eyes from the intense light and took a step back.

"Sara, Queen of Dunbar, my child, why have you come to me alone?" Joseph stated.

"Oh, mighty Joseph, the hour is dire in Dunbar. Andrew and I followed your instructions and the Northlanders have been reunited on the island. True unity has been found, but Andrew's son, Fergus, has had his mind clouded by a treacherous man named Grigori. Fergus has demanded that Andrew give up the throne or there will be war. Andrew and Fergus will not listen to reason, and they are planning on fighting " Sara sadly said.

"Sara, there will always be evil in this world until the return of Christ. This Gregori has a powerful hold over Fergus's mind. Until you cut off the head of the snake, there will be no peace. But I warn you, child, he commands great power and is not to be confronted lightly. His connection to the evil one is strong! Your faith must be strong and don't stray. Look to God for wisdom and strength. Go now, remove the head of the snake and Dunbar will be saved!" Joseph said powerfully.

As Sara walked alone through the forest, she repeated, "Cut off the head. Cut off the head." As she neared the edge of the forest, she felt like she understood.

"I must defeat Grigori and then peace will happen," Sara whispered.

"Oh, God, give me the strength I am going to need. Please save our kingdom and the kingdoms of this island. Let there be peace," she spoke.

Finn looked happy to see her as she emerged from the edge of the trees.

"My queen, I was starting to worry. Come over here by the fire and have some stew. I'm sure you are starved," Finn said.

The two ate quietly by the fire, talking in low tones. It was decided that in the morning they would leave for the Black Hills for Sara had told Finn of her need to find Gregori's quarters. Finn didn't understand the need for this quest, but he obeyed the queen's orders. What neither knew was that they weren't the only ones out under the stars that night, for there was a stranger lurking in the darkness listening to their entire conversation.

After several days of riding, Sara and Finn made it to the outskirts of the Black Hills. Sara asked local villagers if they knew where Grigori's home was located. After several attempts, an older man described the dreary outcast of what was known as the wretchedness of the kingdom. It was in the far southeastern section, where the winds blew constantly, and the land was barren. The man warned the queen that this was a dark, dangerous place. The people living there were uncivilized barbarians and wouldn't hesitate to kill outsiders. Sara looked at Finn with determination and thanked the man. They ate a quick meal and headed out at once. The deeper the two ventured into the Black Hills Kingdom, the more it changed. As they traveled in a southeastern direction, they noticed the land became less fertile, the trees and bushes less full, livestock less plentiful, and the people less friendly. They noticed fewer churches as well.

By nightfall they reached the outskirts of the hamlet
the guide said Grigori lived in. Finn and Sara decided to
get a low fire going and at dawn, they would sneak into
Grigori's lair. When early morning arose, the two got up
and walked toward the tiny village. The first light was
barely hitting the earth and it was hard for the two to de-
cipher which building was Grigori's hut. They noticed that
one hut was much larger than the others, and figured it
was his. Sara cautiously opened the door, making sure not
to make any noises. As the two entered, Sara could feel
the evil emanating throughout the room. Even though it
was still dark, Sara could see unthinkable objects hanging
from the ceiling and walls. There were bones, skulls, tools,
books, and vials of unknown liquids all throughout. A
large cauldron was placed in the middle of the room, and it
was simmering. It truly was a place of extreme wickedness.
Horrible things had been done in this building, and Sara's
body had goosebumps all over it.

"Be careful where you step, Finn, I sense dark and
dangerous pitfalls throughout this room," Sara said.

A loud, evil-sounding laugh then projected through
the room.

"Agh, Sara of Dunbar, so nice of you to visit. My, my,
you are a very determined woman. I will give you this, you
are very brave. Too bad your braveness will be your down-
fall. The Queen of Dunbar's life will end today, and it will
end here, in the den of Grigori!" Grigori evilly stated.

Sara was jolted by Grigori's voice and stepped back,
bumping into Finn.

"Yes, Grigori, it is I, Sara of Dunbar, and I have come
here to rid the earth of your wicked ways. You have harmed
people on this island long enough, it is time for this to end,"
Sara confidently replied.

As Sara was speaking, she could sense Finn approaching from behind. She was expecting the two of them to combat Grigori as a team.

"Finn, go to my left and we will take him on together," Sara said not looking away from Grigori.

But instead of following her orders, Finn was standing behind Sara with a large club held high in the air. Sara could feel something wasn't right, so she turned around to see Finn towering over top of her with the club facing in her direction. He had an evil look on his face and was smiling. She was stunned and knew instantly there wasn't time for her to do anything, so she closed her eyes and awaited the inevitable. She heard a loud thud and opened her eyes. She saw Finn's body on the ground and Pavel standing behind him with a large piece of wood.

"Pavel, what are you doing here?" Sara asked bewildered.

"I have followed the two of you here all the way from Dunbar. I never trusted him, there was something not right with him. I have sworn to protect you, Sara, and I will continue to lay down my life for you. You have shown me the way," Pavel said.

"You fool, Pavel, what are you doing? Finn was my spy who was supposed to kill the queen, but now it can be you. You can't be with those weak, God-loving Dunbarians," Grigori shrieked.

"No, I was with you, but no more. You clouded my mind and convinced me to team up with the Odorans. You put anger in my heart and told me lies. You did the same to Igor and other kings of the Black Hills. But no more, your hold over the minds of the people must end," Pavel bravely stated.

Just then, a dozen of Grigori's wicked followers entered the room and formed a circle around him. Grigori smiled and looked at Sara and Pavel with a smirk.

"Of course, I was the one who pulled the strings of the kings. Behind the scenes, I've been using my powers to control the Black Hills kings and fill their minds with anger and jealousy. Now I have Fergus under my control as well. It has been so easy to sway their simple minds. Pavel, you have chosen your fate. You will die alongside the queen. After Fergus and Andrew's armies have decimated each other, I can step in and control the minds of all the kings on this island. I will bring more destruction and chaos, and the island will be mine!" Grigori laughed.

"Not if I have a say in it!" Sara yelled as she quickly strung an arrow to her bow. She fired at the cauldron, knocking it over, and the contents spread across the floor. Pavel and Sara knocked the candles onto the liquid, and a fire instantly erupted inside the hut. Large explosions and bangs filled the air, and the two ran out of the room as it became engulfed with flames.

"Grab the horses!" Sara excitedly yelled.

The two mounted their horses and sprinted away from the hamlet. As they stormed away, Sara looked behind her. She could see Grigori's hut lighting up the early morning sky, but more importantly, she could see the enemy mounting black menacing-looking horses.

TWELVE

The Protector

As Sara and Pavel were evading Grigori and his assembly of henchmen, the large armies were facing each other at the top of the Plains of Daniel. They squared off against each other about fifty feet away, banging their swords against their shields and shouting loudly. Fergus's army, though smaller in size, had many men from five of the kingdoms. He had convinced several of Dunbar's best soldiers to switch sides, and he had a surprisingly larger coalition of Lancot and Black Hills soldiers standing alongside him than Andrew expected. Each man wore metal armor and had round shields attached to their backs. Maces, clubs, shields, and swords were the weapons of the day. Andrew's army was larger, more experienced, and included the leaders of the kingdoms. They were well-equipped and eager to do battle that day. Andrew trotted out with Elaran to meet Fergus and his second Danilo (from the Black Hills).

"My son, this is your last chance to call off the battle. I don't want to hurt you and kill all these innocent men. Do what's right and leave the battlefield," Andrew stated.

"No, Father, that will not happen today. You have ruled long enough. Your leadership is lacking, and your judgment has diminished. My destiny has been foretold, and I will be king by day's end," Fergus said as he looked into his father's eyes."

"Fool, you've let this despicable creature Grigori take ahold of your mind and you are not thinking straight. You will regret your actions today," Andrew angrily said.

"You'd be willing to kill your own father?" Elaran asked.

"If that is what it takes, yes. I don't enjoy having to do this, but he has left me no choice. Our kingdom and this island need strong leadership, the type of leadership only I can give," Fergus responded.

"So be it, I'm done trying to talk sense into you. Until we meet on the battlefield, my son, God be with you," Andrew sadly stated.

The four rode away from each other, father and son both feeling in their hearts they were doing what their kingdom needed. As Andrew rode back into line he looked down at his soldiers' faces. He could see their determination and loyalty and knew the time was at hand. His emotions were troubled, but he felt like he couldn't back down now. He was part of a moving plot and there was nothing he could do to stop it.

As the two armies were about to engage with each other, Sara and Pavel were riding to the battlefield. They had been riding their horses for days. They were fatigued and their horses were near exhaustion. They had been sprinting ahead of Grigori and his evil henchmen, but the enemy was close behind. In fact, Grigori's group was gaining on them. Arrows and spears were flying dangerously close to Sara and Pavel as they rode on horseback.

"We must do something; they are getting too close to us!" Pavel screamed.

"Do what, we can't stop the horses, they outnumber us ten to one," Sara yelled back.

Both armies looked down from the top of the plains. From their vantage point, they could see clearly for miles. They saw two riders being closely pursued by a dozen men wearing dark cloaks throwing spears at them. The two armies stopped their screaming and shield banging and watched the unfolding chase with intrigue.

Sara knew she had to do something quickly, or Grigori's men would catch them and end their lives. Sara pulled her long, golden cross out of her pocket and held it with one hand. She raised it into the air and prayed as loud as she could.

"Oh, Father, please protect us! Keep us safe from this enemy that's chasing us. Show me the way, give me guidance, and wrap your protective arms around us in our time of need. Please, God, keep us safe and save us!" Sara screamed.

At that moment, the clouds parted, and an immense light shone down upon the riders. The light brightened up the sky, and the armies on top of the plains could see the scene as clearly as looking in a mirror. The light was not only extremely bright but very hot. It didn't seem to affect Sara and Pavel, but Grigori's riders slowed their pursuit to a trot. The light was burning their skin, and they all were shouting out in pain. Sara and Pavel slowed their horses and turned around to witness this puzzling turn of events. The lights had blinded the eyes of their enemies, and they didn't see that they rode right into a pit of quicksand. Horses and men were frantically scrambling to get out of the sticky substance, but the more they moved, the greater the sand tightened around their bodies. Sara watched in amazement as entire bodies slowly were engulfed by the pit. Hands and fingers were the last body parts to be seen before they completely sunk.

"HELP ME! Help me!" Grigori screamed.

Grigori was lying sideways in the pit, with his legs completely submerged. His arms were outstretched as he yelled at Sara.

"Let him die an undignified death, he doesn't deserve to be saved, my queen," Pavel said.

Sara thought for a second, she knew his evil, wicked ways had caused so much strife and destruction for so many people on the island. She wanted to let him die, but she rode toward him in an effort to save him. As she touched his outstretched fingers Grigori's hand slipped away, and he slowly submerged into the quicksand. This evil man was dead, and the island would be free from his destructive plans forever. Sara quickly said a prayer, looked at Pavel, and then they rode off toward the Plains of Daniel, hoping to stop the ensuing civil war.

The men at the summit of the plains looked on with great attentiveness. As Grigori slipped into the sand, men's minds became clear again. It was as if a great cloud was lifted. They all dropped their weapons and tears rolled down their cheeks. Men from both sides walked toward each other and hugged. They started talking with each other and apologizing for their actions. Andrew and Fergus met at the center of the field and embraced. Both men were deeply embarrassed!

"Father, I am so sorry. I don't know what came over me. It was as if someone had control over my mind and I couldn't break this cloud. Please, oh please, can you forgive me?" Fergus said.

"No, my son, it is I that needs forgiveness. I should have never brought this army here, I let anger and stubbornness control me. Will you forgive me?" Andrew stated.

As both men apologized and embraced, they could see the army part and Sara and Pavel came riding into the middle of the men. As soon as Sara entered the circle of men, they all got down on one knee, and in a demonstration of dignity, they looked up at the beautiful queen. Archers, soldiers, clergy, and royals alike, bent a knee to the great queen. Andrew, Elaran, Fergus, and all the kings of the island joined their men and bowed down. All in unison, they said, "The Protector! Sara is the true protector. All hail Sara, the Protector of Dunbar!"

Six months later, on a beautiful sunlit spring day, in the halls of the great Woodendale castle, all the royals from each of the six kingdoms were standing together. King Elaran from Woodendale, Magnus from the Northland, Sergio from the Black Hills, Addison from Watertown, the elderly Afron from Lancot, and of course, Andrew from Dunbar. It had been agreed upon after the civil war was averted, the six kings should meet to draw up a covenant. This new covenant would describe the laws and agreements amongst the kingdoms. This would further emphasize the unity and peace that had been created. Each man was smiling from end to end as they all signed the last page of the covenant. To formalize the covenant, they all agreed to make a new tapestry that ALL six kingdoms would keep in their great halls. A tapestry that would show all six kings in a circle, grasping each other's arms. As Andrew looked around at his fellow kings, his friends, he smiled. He looked over at his beautiful wife, Sara, and smiled even more. He thought of his life, his family and upbringing, his adventures. He couldn't be any happier than at that moment. The island was at peace, it was unified, and his family was safe. It was a great day to be King of Dunbar!

A
SHORT STORY
of
DUNCAN
THE STURDY

A Short Story of
Duncan the Sturdy

In the time of darkness, before Andrew was even born, when all kingdoms on the island were weary of each other, comes a tale of unbelievable strength and courage. The island's five kingdoms were in turmoil. The Kingdoms of Woodendale and Lancot had a delicate truce after spending a decade fighting over territory both believed belonged to them. Watertown, the port city that all kingdoms relied on for imports, had been hoarding all incoming items, not wanting to share with perceived ungracious kingdoms. And all the kingdoms were at war with the Black Hills, a kingdom of unruly, angry people. Duncan's people, the Kingdom of Dunbar, were constantly at war with this dark kingdom. This is where our tale begins, a dreary, rain-soaked day in the land between Dunbar and the Black Hills.

"Men, the rain is getting heavier. It is getting harder to see and our horses are tired and wet. I think we should stop here and make shelter. We can try moving on when the storm slows. Don't be discouraged, warriors from Dunbar, we will carry out our mission, we will bring revenge to the evil hordes of our enemy," Duncan confidently said.

They all stared at him with the utmost respect. This tall, imposing man was in his prime physically. He was over six feet tall with bulging arm and leg muscles. He had piercing green eyes and long, reddish-blonde hair, which many men envied. His brother, King James, had given Duncan the title Commander in Chief of Dunbar. Duncan oversaw the Dunbarian army, and his men obeyed his authority completely. He had proven himself in battle over the past two years for he was fearless yet wise. His determination brought confidence to his soldiers who looked to him for guidance and wisdom.

Duncan was leading a small group of around fifty soldiers on a scouting mission to find the whereabouts of the Black Hills army. Their orders were to locate the enemy but not engage. A larger army would be brought in from the rear to confront and destroy the enemy after its location was discovered.

After making a dry shelter, the men sat around Duncan waiting for him to share one of his amusing stories. Duncan looked back and forth at his men who were staring up at this imposing man. Just as Duncan was to speak, a twig snapped. The men all looked up and before they could move, a swarm of Black Hills soldiers stormed through the camp. Unsuspecting Dunbarian soldiers were being attacked with clubs and spears as the enemy soldiers were screaming like banshees. As Duncan looked around, he saw his comrades being pinned down on the ground and clubbed. Men tried fleeing into the woods, but they were chased down by the swarming, wicked enemy. The enemy was brutal, for they were taking no prisoners. Dunbarian men were being struck down and slaughtered. Duncan reached for his sword but in the chaos, he couldn't find it.

His captain, named Logan, grabbed Duncan's arm and yelled, "Follow me, I have my sword with me." The two of them raced toward the woods, but a group of around twenty enemy soldiers blocked their entrance. As the two turned to flee in the other direction, several of the enemy jumped on Duncan's back and started choking him. He fell to the ground with nine men holding onto him. As he looked up, he saw Logan battling enemy fighters on all sides. An arrow flew into Logan's chest as he approached a large Black Hills soldier. Logan fell to the ground, completely surrounded. In an instant, they ended his life.

"NO!" screamed Duncan.

As Duncan struggled with men holding him down on the ground, he looked up to see a large Black Hills man walking toward him. The man got within five feet of Duncan and bent down to eye level. He chuckled and lifted Duncan's head.

"Oh, the great Duncan, who's at my feet now?" yelled the man.

"Let me up and we'll see who's at each other's feet! And stranger, you are being rude, you never introduced yourself to me," Duncan replied.

"I am Mykola, son of Ivan, the high-ranking general of King Vladimir. I have just killed all your men, and now you will suffer." He erupted with evil laughter.

Mykola took a large block hammer from his belt and smacked Duncan in the face. Duncan wearily looked up before losing consciousness. The last thing he saw was Mykola taking a dagger from his belt.

When Duncan awoke, he felt nauseous. His head ached and his muscles were sore. He moved his arms and legs, but they were chained to a wall.

"They must be holding me as a prisoner in this God-forsaken land," Duncan whispered to himself. "This must be some sort of dungeon."

The lair was dimly lit and very large. It was a circular room at least fifty feet wide with a low ceiling. Duncan noticed he could see his breath for it was very chilly and damp.

Duncan took the next several minutes to get his bearings. It took a while for his eyes to adjust to the low light, but he thought he saw another prisoner at the opposite end of the dungeon.

"You, over there, speak to me. I am Duncan, son of James from the Kingdom of Dunbar. Who are you?" Duncan asked.

After a long pause, Duncan could hear the man rattling his chains. In a very low, soft voice Duncan could hear the stranger begin to speak.

"It is so nice to hear from another person. I haven't seen or heard from another person besides the guards in almost ten years. The Black Hills captured me years ago and locked me in this dreaded place. You know me, Duncan, for it is I, Callum."

"Callum? Callum! Is it really you, we all thought you were dead. You've been here for the last ten years?"

"Yes, Duncan, it is I. I'm sure you all thought I was dead, but no I am alive, if you call my existence the last ten years living. These horrible people have barely kept me alive in this damp, dingy dungeon. They barely feed me and don't allow me another coat to wear in this cold place. I've almost perished several times, but God has kept me alive."

"Why are they doing this to you?" Duncan asked.

"They try every month to get me to recant and disavow my faith. They tell me if I do so, they will release me. I don't believe them, and I would never recant. I'd rather die than recant. I tell them this every time but they only yell at me and hit me. I've been praying for a miracle for a long time, seeing you makes my heart happy. I haven't had much hope in a long time," Callum stated.

As Duncan prepared to respond, both men heard loud voices coming down the stairs. The large metal door to the dungeon opened and several men came walking into the room. They were wearing their armor and were heavily armed. They walked briskly over toward Duncan. Mykola looked into Duncan's eyes and spoke.

"Commander of the Dunbar army, as you can see you are our prisoner now. Your name has been spoken amongst our people for a while now, it is nice to finally have captured you. Too many of our men have perished because of your fearless attitude. My master, the great King of the Black Hills is willing to make you a deal. Instead of just killing you as we did your soldiers, we will give you a chance to leave this dungeon and return to Dunbar unimpeded."

"What trick is this? You can't be serious!" Duncan yelled back.

"No, I'm not lying. Here is your challenge, a challenge we've given to several prisoners over the years. You see, we have another dungeon room where we hold a creature we call Barclay. Barclay is a monster bear, as tall as this ceiling and as wide as a wagon. He is ferocious and aggressive for we antagonize him with sticks and deprive food from him daily. The deal is this, if you can fight Barclay and defeat him, you will be free to go. If instead he kills you, we will allow him to eat you. This is your deal, and on my honor, we will abide by it. If you choose not to accept this deal, we will kill you and stake your head for all to see." Mykola chuckled.

Duncan thought for a while, and then responded, "I don't feel like I have much of a choice. I will accept your challenge. Can you please give me some nourishment, so I have a better chance?"

Mykola laughed and laughed for a whole minute. He pointed toward a guard who left the room but entered a minute later with a plate of food. As he approached, Mykola grabbed the plate from him. Looking into Duncan's eyes, he dropped the plate on the ground and the food scattered in several directions. Mykola laughed again and ordered the guards to hold Duncan as he landed a blow across his face..

"You expect any mercy from us, you are mistaken, royalty of Dunbar. For too long your people have held its boot upon our kingdom. Now it is our turn for revenge, and we will get it. I can't wait to watch him tear you from limb to limb." Mykola then spit into Duncan's face and walked out of the dungeon with the guards, leaving Duncan and Callum alone.

"Duncan, Duncan, are you ok?" Callum weakly said.

Duncan lifted his head up from the ground with blood trickling down his face. He was bruised and exhausted. Before he replied to Callum, he noticed something on the ground. Two feet in front of him was a two-inch-long wooden spike. It was really sharp and thick enough to do damage. One of the guards must have dropped it accidentally, and Duncan quickly grabbed it and hid it inside his sleeve.

"I'm okay, Callum. I will meet my fate today. Please pray with me and then I will rest before they return. Will you say the Lord's Prayer with me?" Duncan asked.

"Yes, are you ready, my friend?" Callum replied.

In unison, they both said, "Our Father, who art in heaven, hallowed be thy name; thy kingdom come; thy will be done; on earth as it is in heaven. Give us this day our daily bread. And forgive us our trespasses, as we forgive those who trespass against us. And lead us not into temptation; but deliver us from evil."

Callum let Duncan rest and the room was quiet. After about an hours' time had gone by, Duncan looked into the sky and prayed to God to give him the strength of Sampson and wisdom of Solomon.

Just then the door opened. Several men came into the room holding a stick with a chain attached to the bear's neck. They were pulling with all their might as the bear was roaring and thrashing. As the bear entered the room, Duncan was taken aback by the sheer size of it. It towered over any human being and was so thick. It took twelve men pulling the chains to move Barclay. Mykola entered the room after the bear was safely escorted inside. He looked over at Duncan with a stern face and no emotion.

"Your time is up, royalty of Dunbar. We will loosen your chains in a minute. If you make any moves toward any of my men, we will shoot arrows into you and feed you to this monster, do you understand?" Mykola shouted.

They let Duncan free from his chains and positioned the bear, so it faced Duncan. It was salivating and roaring intensely as it looked at Duncan. As the last iron ring was loosened from its neck, it rushed toward Duncan. It thrashed with its mighty paws and tried biting down on Duncan's neck. Duncan dodged the mighty bear and moved away from it. He felt a strange calmness as warmth flowed through him. He slipped the small spike from his sleeve and held it in his right hand.

The bear charged again, and this time Duncan took a full swing at Barclay. He hit the bear with all his might and the bear shrieked in pain. The spike had hit its target for it was stuck in the bear's left eye. Blood was gushing down the bear's face, so Duncan quickly raced to get behind it. He jumped on its back and circled his massive arms around the bear's neck and squeezed. He held on with all his might as the bear tried knocking him off his back. Duncan didn't relent. The bear dropped down on its knees and Duncan held on with all his might.

He whispered, "Oh, mighty Barclay, I regret having to do this to you. I don't want to kill you, but these evil people give me no choice. Soon you will be in the afterlife, I thank you for your life."

After several minutes, the bear breathed its last breath. Duncan released the bear and stood up. He was shaking from using so much energy and could barely stand. The Black Hills guards entered the room and rushed toward Duncan with weapons drawn.

"Well, well, the stories are true. The mighty Duncan has the strength of ten men. You have done the unthinkable, you defeated Barclay. No man has ever come close to doing this," Mykola said.

"Now release me, we had a deal," Duncan shouted.

"We did have a deal, but you cheated. You used a weapon, for I see the wood spike in the bear's eye. Your treachery broke our agreement. We will not let you go; we will kill you," Mykola stated.

At that moment the guards all rushed Duncan and repeatedly attacked him. Mykola looked down at the exhausted and suffering Dunbarian.

"I almost feel sorry for you for you are truly a great warrior. But your time on Earth is fleeting, and our kingdom will rejoice in the morning. We will behead you and let the ravens pick at your body," Mykola sneered.

Duncan looked up and made sure he had eye contact.

"My God will save me. I will not perish tomorrow for my time is not ready," Duncan hoarsely stated.

"YOUR GOD! Where is your God at this moment? You fool, there is no God. I spit at that notion," Mykola yelled before spitting in front of Duncan. He swiftly exited the room and slammed the door shut.

Duncan slowly rose and walked over to where Callum was lying. He sat down next to him and put his arm around him.

"What can I do now, old friend? They promised my release and it was all a lie! I defeated the beast, but it was all a lie! How can we escape from this horrible dungeon? What am I to do?" Duncan slowly said.

Callum looked into Duncan's eyes and put his hands on his face.

"We will do the only thing that we can, my friend. We will pray, we will put all our faith in our God, surrender to him and he will find a way. Proverbs 3:5-6 states that we trust in the Lord with all our heart, and do not lean on our own understanding. In all our ways acknowledge him, and he will make straight our paths."

Duncan held his hands and nodded in agreement. They both prayed, opening their hearts and souls to the Lord.

"Duncan, you need to rest. Please sleep and I will pray through the night. God will find a way, I promise. You were brought here for a reason," Callum stated. Duncan did as he was told and fell into a deep sleep. He slept for several hours but was roused from his sleep by shaking. He quickly stood up but fell over as the dungeon was shaking and vibrating.

"An earthquake!" Duncan yelled.

The room shook and stones fell from the walls and ceiling. Duncan fell on top of Callum and shielded him. The earthquake was mighty and lasted for several minutes. Callum's chains broke away from the wall and the door to the dungeon opened all on its own.

"This is our chance! We must leave immediately," Duncan said to Callum.

"I am too weak; I would slow you down. Go, leave me, and go. Get your freedom from this dreaded place!" Callum said.

"I will not leave you. I was put in this dreaded place for a reason! I am here to free you and free you I will," Duncan yelled.

He quickly snatched up Callum and placed him on his thick back.

"WE are getting out of here, hold on tight," Duncan shouted.

Duncan ran toward the open dungeon door and jumped through it with Callum on his back. He noticed both guards were lying under large chunks of the wall so there was nobody obstructing his exit. He leapt the stairs taking two or three at a time, dodging the chunks of wall in the stairway. The farther he went up, the lighter and warmer it was getting. He reached the top of the stairway and noticed the guard lying on the ground with wounds from the earthquake. The guard looked up at Duncan but was too injured to say a word. Duncan noticed the hallway was only about fifteen feet long, so he sprinted with all his might praying to God for safety and strength.

When he exited the castle, he could see the damage from the earthquake up close. Buildings, barns, and trees were lying all over the ground. As he looked around there were men, women, and children lying wounded or dead. In the middle of the street was a healthy, brown-colored horse. It had no saddle, no markings at all. It was all alone, no master holding on to its reins. It stared at Duncan as if it were saying "Come to me." It whipped its neck, so its long thick mane wisped in the air. He ran toward the horse and hoisted Callum up before jumping on its back. The horse didn't flinch and waited for Duncan to steady himself.

"Go, go! Ride like the wind, my friend!" Duncan howled.

The horse took off as Duncan held on to its neck with all his might. Callum clung to Duncan, and they sped off in the direction of Dunbar. With the chaos of the earthquake, they were unimpeded as they raced through the countryside. They raced without any intrusions for hours and hours. On the third day, they reached the outskirts of the Dunbar kingdom where the guards stopped them. Duncan the Sturdy had done it.

"Now how do we know this tale is true? Well, it is because I, Callum the Lost, am recounting the story of Duncan the Sturdy. As God as my witness, I lived and observed this tale. The man who killed the bear, saved the forgotten priest, and rode out of the Black Hills on a strapping horse. It all happened; it is all true. May God bless Duncan the Sturdy!"